A Mail Order Bride For Charlie

The Carson Brothers of Kansas
Book One

By Carré White

This is a work of fiction. Names, characters, places, and incidents either are the product of the author's imagination or are used fictitiously, and any resemblance to any persons, living or dead, business establishments, events, or locales is entirely coincidental.

A MAIL ORDER BRIDE FOR CHARLIE

Published by Love Lust Story
Copyright © 2014 by Carré White
Cover art by Erin Dameron-Hill
ISBN: 149534097X
ISBN-13: 978-1495340970

First Print Edition: February 2014

Books by Carré White

The Carson Brothers of Kansas

———

A Mail Order Bride for Charlie
A Mail Order Bride for Bronson
A Mail Order Bride for Wyatt
A Mail Order Bride for Grant

The Colorado Brides Series

———

An Unexpected Widow
An Unexpected Bride
An Unexpected Annulment
An Unexpected Mother
An Unexpected Love

The Arizona Brides Series

———

An Audacious Spitfire

Sonoran Nights

CONTENTS

One

The Carson Ranch, Kansas, June 1869

I was the youngest of four brothers, the two eldest having been through the war, while Grant and I had been too young to participate, which was a blessing. Our pa, Chuck Carson, who was a Free-State man, had moved us west from Massachusetts, but he lost his life in a skirmish with a small army of Missourians. Our mother had been widowed, although my older brothers, Bronson and Wyatt had taken over the farm before setting out to fight in the war.

When they returned, they weren't the same, and, although our farm prospered, first from wheat and corn, then from the stockyards, my older brothers had changed. It was rumored that Bronson had taken to robbery, while Wyatt enjoyed wild nights at various saloons. Grant was fond of the ladies, romancing a married woman in town, whose husband was frequently away on cattle business. My mother, Maggie, beside herself with worry over her wayward sons, had taken matters into her own hands, and it wasn't until a day ago that I realized just how desperate she had become.

"Charlie," she had said. "You're such a good boy. You're the only one of your brothers I can count on. I've something I need you to do for me."

I had been about to saddle a horse, standing in the stable with the bridle in my hands. "Yes, Ma?" *Lord, what is it now?*

She stood before me in a faded purple dress with an apron tied around her waist. "I've…been, well, I've an errand for you, son."

"I gotta check the fence. We got some escapees."

"I know, but once you've done that, I…have something important that needs tending to."

"Can't Grant do it?"

"He's been gone for two days." Her expression darkened. "I know what he's been doing. I know all about Mrs. Forrester. Nothing good will come from being associated with that woman. The rumors are true, I'm afraid."

"He's a grown man. You can't tell a grown man what to do."

"Why did my boys have to turn out so wild?

What have I done to deserve this? We never should've left home. It was a mistake moving west."

"Pa wanted more land, you know that. He worked hard to build the farm. He did better than most." She had yet to forgive him for his part in the skirmish that had resulted in his death, but…that was years ago. Those, who had committed the murder, were now gone too. They had paid for their crimes.

"I need you to go to Topeka. I have something important arriving at the station that needs to be picked up."

"I'm busy." I placed the leather straps around the horse's muzzle. "Ask Cutter or Derrick to do it."

"I can't. This is a delicate matter, Charlie. I need someone I can trust."

"I'll look for Grant later. He can take care of it."

"That won't do. The thing that's arriving *is* for Grant. It's a sort of…present."

I glanced over my shoulder, feeling a growing sense of irritation. "I ain't no errand boy, Ma. Make him get his own stuff, that lazy cuss." I placed the saddle pad high on the horse's withers.

"Oh, goodness."

"Derrick's got nothin' going. He's dithering around in the bunkhouse. He needs a job."

"I have something to tell you. I know you'll be angry with me, but it's too late now. The wheels are in motion."

I stared at her, my mouth turning down. *Oh, what now?* "What have you done?"

"I've taken matters into my own hands. Your brother needs a wife, Charlie. There are plenty of women back east, lookin' for a fresh start. There are advertisements for mail order brides in the newspaper every week. I—"

Then it dawned on me, what she had done. "Oh, Lordy!" I barked with laughter, not being able to help myself. "You didn't."

"I've begun a pleasant correspondence with a lovely young woman from New York."

"Let me guess; she's showin' up on the afternoon train."

"Yes, she is."

Chuckling, I shook my head, laughing at the insanity of the situation. "It ain't gonna work. You just wasted your time and energy on nothin'." I glanced at her. "Did you have to pay for the ticket?"

"I…did, but she thinks Grant's responsible. I've been sending letters…but I made them sound like something Grant would say."

I had finished with the saddle, fastening the front clinch. "Boy, oh, boy. He's not gonna be too happy about that." I snorted with laughter, imagining Grant returning home tonight to face his future wife, although he would never marry this woman. "You gone and done it now, Ma."

"Not really. I've only hurried the matrimonial process. But…" She looked worried, wringing her hands.

"What?"

"She expects to be married…today."

This announcement sent me over the edge, as I hooted uncontrollably. I tossed my head back, while my belly clenched with the force of my amusement. *Oh, tarnation! There's no way on God's green earth Grant will marry this woman today or ever.*

"This isn't funny, you blockhead! This is important, Charlie! I've played around with this poor woman's life, promising her the moon and the stars. Now she's nearly here, and there's no Grant."

"Did you romance her sweetly in those letters, Ma?" Another fit of laughter had me in its grips, as I doubled over. "You sure have a way with words. Bet you wrote some poetry too, eh?" Tears were in my eyes, but the laughter would not abate.

"Get a grip, Charlie! I need you to retrieve her. Tell her the wedding's been slightly delayed, and bring her home."

I shook my head. "Of all the crazy things you've done. This one sure takes the cake."

She remained unapologetic. "When Grant sees

her, he'll make an offer. I have it on good authority
that she's handsome."

"I'm sure." I doubted it, but why should I
throw water on a perfectly good fire?

"Will you go get her?"

"You're the one doin' the courting. Why don't
you get her?" This idea was so ridiculous; another
fit of laugher escaped, until my belly ached.
"Lordy, this has been fun. Haven't laughed this
much in ages."

"You knucklehead!" Anger blazed in her look
now. She was all fired up. "I've not had an easy go
of life, son; you know that. Your father's death and
the war have dealt us blows we never recovered
from. You're the only one I can count on in this
family. You're the only one who won't let me
down. You stayed to help and make the farm
prosper. All I ask is that you go to the train station
and retrieve this woman. Is that so hard?"

"I got no qualms about pickin' stuff up, but I
can't look at this person and lie to her. She came
out here on good faith, and you've been lying the
entire time. What do you think she'll do when she
finds out you faked those letters?" My hands went
to my hips. "She'll hightail it on outta here, is what
she'll do."

"She can't. It's a one way ticket."

My belly rumbled again. I began to cough; the
sound was loud enough to upset the horse. I patted

her flank. "There now, Sonny. Sorry about that. Don't pay me no mind. I'm just tryin' not to die over here."

"Will you get the woman?"

"You mean, will I help perpetuate the lie?"

"Not for long. Just bring her here, and I'll explain everything."

"Why not go get her yourself? Tell her what you told me, and let her decide what to do. Give her the fare, and she'll get back on the train and go home. It would be for the best."

"I don't want that! She's the perfect woman for Grant. I didn't make promises for nothing, Charlie. Once Grant sees her, he'll fall in love."

"Just like that, huh?" My smile had yet to falter. "That's all it takes?"

"Oh, stop making fun of me. I raised you better than that."

"Yeah, you did. I got me a fine conscience that's telling me what you did was underhanded and manipulative. You lied to this poor woman, and you're lying to Grant. The only person payin' the piper on this one will be you." I pointed a finger at her. "You're gonna have a lotta explaining to do."

"That's fair. I'll take that. I deserve it, but it's high time my boys are married and settled. I've raised four of the most ungrateful wretches ever. Your older brothers are nothin' but wastrels. They came back from the war all messed up in their heads with bellies full of whiskey. I've lost hope that either of them will ever marry. Then Grant took up with a married woman! Oh, the shame. And they're hardly discreet. I'll do anything to get him away from that cheating, conniving Mrs. Forrester. That woman should be ashamed of herself for carrying on like that."

"It ain't up to you to be the judge."

"No, but it won't happen with *my* son!"

"Grant's a big boy. He makes his own decisions."

"He's not had a father around for guidance. Chuck would've never stood for this sort of behavior. He would've taken a firm hand to him and set him straight."

"That worked real well for Wyatt and Bronson," I remarked dryly.

"Oh, those boys." She closed her eyes. "I can only concern myself right now with the ones worth savin'. Grant's not too far gone...yet."

"You've given up on Wyatt and Bronson then? Are they as good as dead to you?"

"No, of course not. I haven't seen either of them in months. I check the paper every week to see..."

My humor had vanished. "To see what?"

"The arrests and the obituaries. I expect to read all about it there."

She had a point, and I would not be able to argue with her on that score, although I had seen Wyatt last week. He had come to town on a job, looking the worse for wear. "What am I gonna tell this woman?"

"Just say that Grant's been waylaid and the wedding's been slightly postponed."

"Is she travelin' with a chaperone?"

"With an elderly couple, but they'll part ways in Topeka."

"Then she'll be at the house without a chaperone."

"I'm the chaperone."

"This harebrained scheme ain't gonna work. You're just delaying the inevitable. Grant's not gonna marry this woman. He's not ready for marriage, period. None of us are."

"You're still young."

"I ain't *that* young. Twenty-four is gettin' up there."

"I've...oh, never mind."

Something unpleasant settled in my belly. "You don't plan on bringin' one of these ladies out for me, do you?"

"No, of course not." She wouldn't look me in the eye.

"Mother?"

"Just go and get Rebecca Hart, and we'll discuss this later."

"There's nothin' left to discuss." I glared at her, feeling less than thrilled with the notion of having to lie to a stranger. This deception was beneath my mother. It was beneath all of us. "You never really answered me. You're not plannin' on bringing one of these women out here for me, are you?"

"No, honey, I'm not."

"You sure? You look like you're hiding something."

"Stop it, Charlie."

"You were plannin' on it, weren't you? You were gonna set me up with some stranger." My amusement had disappeared, replaced with fuming irritation. This would be how Grant felt once he heard the news. Our mother had put us in an impossible situation.

"I'll not do it to you. I…promise."

"This won't work out the way you think. She's not gonna marry Grant. She's gonna take one look around and skedaddle on outta here."

"Maybe, maybe not. I've faith that I chose the right person for your brother. She's a lovely woman, who's in need of a family. I've seen a drawing of her. She's perfectly proportioned. The nose is just right."

I wanted to laugh at the ridiculousness of the situation, but I couldn't. "I've got fences to check, but I'll leave for Topeka later."

Her smile was filled with relief and gratitude. "Oh, thank goodness. I knew I could count on you."

"You're gonna pay for this. It ain't gonna end well; mark my words."

"Things will turn out splendidly, Charlie. Don't you worry about a thing."

I snorted in reply. She couldn't be more wrong about that.

Two

Outside of Topeka, Kansas
I had taken a chance…and here I was. I was due to arrive in Topeka within an hour, having traveled from New York by train. It was my first trip from home, although I had nothing to go back to now. I had been living with my sister, but that arrangement had turned inhospitable.

I adored my sister, Collette, greatly, but I found her husband intimidating. There was something in his manner that made my skin crawl, especially when he brushed up against me, which seemed to happen far too often for my liking. I had been taking care of my mother, who had become ill, but, after she died, the landlord made it clear he wanted me gone. I had moved into Collette's house to mind her children. After discovering an advertisement in the newspaper for mail order brides, I had written to the agency on impulse, and now, six months later, I was going to meet my future husband. This had been the perfect solution to all my problems.

Never having had an adventure before, I relished the idea of traveling to the Wild West and beginning a new life away from the over crowdedness of the city and the struggle to make ends meet. The hustle and bustle of New York, with its busy thoroughfares, noise, and filth, was far behind me now. My sister had begged me not to go, but, after I had shared the letters I had received from Grant Carson, she had agreed that he was an exceptional man. Not only were the letters surprisingly articulate and sweet, but his hopes and dreams were aligned with my own—almost identically.

Falling in love with someone through correspondence was something I never anticipated, but I knew now that it was possible. The depth of feeling and desire he had expressed so eloquently, had touched me deeply. I wasn't normally prone to romantic flights of fancy, but the snippets of poetry had been my undoing. They were simple, yet moving, giving me a glimpse into the inner workings of his soul. The man I was about to marry felt things deeply, he cared deeply, and I could not be happier about having met him.

"We're close now," said Mrs. Aberdeen.

My attention had been out the window at the brownish vista that stretched out to the horizon. "Yes. Very soon."

"Are you nervous?"

Mrs. Aberdeen and her husband, Russell, were my traveling companions. They were an elderly couple, who had decided to join their children in Topeka. I would be traveling on to the town of Elm Hill, near where Grant Carson lived without them.

Was I nervous? "I'm fine. Are you overjoyed? You're about to see your grandchildren."

"Oh, yes. We're thrilled, my dear. It's been three years since our youngest headed west. Now we'll all be in the same place together."

I was happy for her, as she had spoken about her family during the trip, especially at dinner last evening in St. Louis, where we had spent the night. "You won't have to wait long then."

"But the true excitement lies with you. You're about to meet your husband. Nothing could compare to the thrill of that momentous event. You must be beside yourself with nerves."

"Not yet. Maybe once the station comes into view."

The train rocked gently, while the sound of a crying baby had risen above the din. Not being able to afford the luxury of a parlor car, the Aberdeen's and I were in coach, which lacked space and amenities. I envied those a car over, as they sat in comfortable leather seats, while being attended to by a porter. My future husband had purchased the tickets, and I understood that he was a man of simple means. I would be a farmer's wife before the day was over. I had been brought up modestly; my father had died when I was young, leaving my mother to take care of my sister and I. When I should have attended socials, meeting bachelors, I was at home with my mother instead, but she had succumbed to sickness despite these efforts.

"You'll write often, won't you, my dear?" asked Mrs. Aberdeen. "I want to hear all about your husband and his family. Perhaps, we can have supper together? We'll be in Topeka now for good. Whenever you come this way, please call on us."

"That would be lovely."

Mr. Aberdeen strolled down the aisle; his sack coat was unbuttoned, revealing a vest and tie. "We're almost there, ladies."

"She's very excited to see Mr. Carson."

"I'm sure she is." He sat next to his wife. "I've had a nice walk through all the cars. I sure do envy 'em in the sleeping car. It must be nice to take a nap for an hour." He yawned. "I could use one."

The shrill sound of a whistle drowned out our conversation, signifying the approach to the station. I stared out the window, hoping to catch a glimpse of something other than grassland.

"Do you see anything?" asked Mrs. Aberdeen.

"No, not yet."

"This must be it." Mr. Aberdeen withdrew a silver watch from his pocket. "Yes, we're nearly on time. How about that?" His grin revealed yellowed and uneven teeth. "Like clockwork."

I craned my neck to catch a glimpse of the illusive station, and, as I watched, the outer edges of a building came into view. "I see it!" A rush of nervous energy coursed through my veins, leaving me slightly dizzy. The thought that I would meet my future husband within minutes had me suddenly questioning this impulsive decision.

I had lain in bed at night, pondering my life and what would become of me. I could not stay at my sister's house, and I had failed to form a relationship with a man. My options were few. I could work as a seamstress or in a factory for low wages or travel out west to marry a stranger. This had been the most appealing of the choices.

"The poor girl looks petrified," said Mrs. Aberdeen. She touched my gloved hand. "It's going to be just fine. I know you've chosen wisely, my dear. You'll learn to love Mr. Carson, and you'll have a passel of children. Any man who can't see how beautiful you are is a fool."

"Oh, you don't have to say that." I was aware that my looks weren't terrible, but I would never call myself a beauty. "I'm acceptable enough, I'm sure. I just…" I bit my lip, "I pray we have a connection. I suppose it's too late to worry about that now."

"I'm sure you will."

The occupants of the car had begun to gather their things; jackets were buttoned, while children's shoes were tied. The crying baby was quiet for the moment, while several men folded newspapers. Women fussed with their hair, pushing loose strands back into their bonnets. I felt self-conscious for a moment, worrying that I looked too plain, but my traveling outfit was reasonably new, the skirts flared, while a beige blouse was hidden beneath a tight-fitting bodice. I had packed a rather heavy bag, which held all of my worldly possessions, two changes of clothing, several chemises and drawers, three pairs of stockings and a nightgown. There was a jacket for winter as well, along with several bonnets and frilly caps. The boots I wore were my only shoes, yet they were just a season old and nearly broken in.

"Topeka!" shouted the porter, who strolled down the aisle, wearing a crisp white shirt and vest. "Topeka! Mind your step!"

"Well, this is it," murmured Mrs. Aberdeen. "We'll wait for you until your fiancé arrives, my dear. We won't abandon you."

For that I was grateful. "Thank you."

The locomotive came to a screeching halt, as a gust of vaporous air drifted before the window. Everyone sprang to their feet, hurrying for the doors, while Mr. and Mrs. Aberdeen waited patiently, walking with me towards the exit.

Summer had yet to arrive, but the layers of clothing I wore had heated me to the core, producing a fine film of moisture on my forehead. I caught sight of myself in the window, seeing a slim young woman in a burgundy dress and straw bonnet. I had tried my best to make a good first impression, hoping that my future husband would not find me disappointing. Having spent most of my life indoors, I was as fair as ivory soap, my skin clear, without a hint of freckles. I'd had them as a child, but they had disappeared over the years.

"I'll take that," said Mr. Aberdeen, reaching for my bag, allowing me to negotiate the steps. "There you are."

"Thank you, sir." When my feet were on the wooden platform, I reclaimed the bag, gazing around at the people who quickly dispersed. I knew what my fiancé looked like from the detailed description he had given me, but no one bore any resemble to it. "I suppose he'll be here shortly."

"I'm hiring a cab," said Mr. Aberdeen. "I'll be inside but a moment."

"I had hoped one of our children would greet us," she said, squinting in the sunlight. "But we couldn't be clear on when we'd be arriving."

I craned my neck, staring at people. "I'm going to look around. I'm sure Mr. Carson will be here any moment. Can you mind my bag?"

"Of course."

I was eager to wander to the other side of the platform, where I spied wagons and carriages. People were loading their belonging onto conveyances, while others hired cabs. The buildings in the distance held my attention, the center of town visible. An assemblage of wooden structures connected by a lengthy boardwalk graced either side of the street. There were dozens of businesses, dry goods, meat markets, and a saddle shop, with others further down. It was a dusty, rustic-looking place, and entirely what I had been expecting.

Removing a white handkerchief from a pocket, I dabbed at my face and neck, feeling the affects of the sun upon my shoulders. This wouldn't be my home, as my fiancé's ranch was nearly two hours away. It was heartening to know that we weren't that far from civilization, although Topeka hardly qualified. We were on the edge of the great frontier, where the railways had yet to extend, but it was just a matter of time, as new tracks were laid every day.

"By golly," I whispered to myself. "This is the boldest thing I've ever done."

As the wagons and carriages began to disappear, the passengers setting out for other destinations, I remained at the edge of the platform, eyeing the circular drive before the station, wondering when my fiancé would appear. A woman carrying a small white dog stepped onto a carriage, while her husband spoke with the driver. Once they had pulled away, it revealed a wagon occupied by a lone man. He seemed to be waiting for someone. Curious, I took several steps in his direction. His dress was casual, denim trousers and a brown tow shirt, tucked into a thick leather belt with a holster. He wasn't dressed for travel, as the other men on the train had been. A wide brimmed hat hid most of his face, casting shadows all the way to his chin.

The description I had been given did not match this man. He was of medium stature, not tall and thin, as described, and his hair was longish, hanging over the collar of his shirt. The color was wrong as well, a honey-blonde instead of nearly black. I sighed, not wanting to give into the rising sense of panic that had gripped me.

"He's not here," I murmured to myself. "Oh, goodness."

Three

I had arrived at the station at four o'clock sharp. On the drive out, I had cursed my mother repeatedly, calling her some rather colorful names, but I was by myself and no one was the wiser, although Sonny had gotten an earful. It irritated me that I would have to tell some strange woman that I was not her intended. Not only that, but Grant wasn't even aware of this circumstance and the events that had been put in motion concerning him.

"Maggie sure has some gall," I muttered, while I waited outside the train station. The reluctance I felt at having to be the bearer of bad news and wasting several hours of my day, had left me in a foul mood. "Where the heck are you, lady? Don't make me come get you."

I had been one of the first to arrive, stopping

nearest to the station, but a horde of wagons and carriages had surrounded me, limiting the view. Not feeling in any hurry to face Rebecca Hart, I had sat waiting, hoping against all hope that she had not been on the train. What sane woman would travel this far to marry a stranger? A handsome woman didn't need to go to such lengths to find a husband.

"She must be especially ugly," I whispered under my breath.

As the wagons pulled away, one by one, the view of the platform was wide open, exposing a lone woman standing with her hands clasped before her. I had seen her earlier, but thought nothing of it, as she was young and pretty. There was an older couple behind her that stood waiting with luggage at their feet. Chewing on a lengthy piece of straw, I remained where I was, cursing my mother for sending me on a fool's errand. I had a long list of things I needed to do, and now they would have to wait until tomorrow.

Removing my hat, I drove fingers through my hair, feeling the dampness of perspiration. I should have waited beneath a tree, not out in the open like this. The woman on the platform seemed to find me interesting then, because her stare was steady. She wandered in my direction.

Rebecca Hart had not made the train. I would wait another five minutes and hightail it on home.

"Sir," said a soft voice.

"Yep."

"I…I'm waiting for someone."

"Me too."

I stepped down from the wagon, stretching my legs. Not relishing the idea of making small talk with a stranger, I stared at my boots, thinking the woman would move on. When she remained where she was, I met her gaze, staring into a pair of deep brown eyes, the kind with thick, black lashes around them. It was like falling into a pool of liquid chocolate. Skin, white as milk, lay shaded beneath the brim of a straw hat.

"I'm waiting for Grant Carson. Do you know him?"

A piece of the straw ended up in my throat, because I had gasped at that announcement. A fit of coughing took over, while my eyes began to water.

"Oh, goodness. Are you all right?"

"Gee willikers!"

"Do you know him?"

"You could say that."

"Is something the matter? Is there some reason he wasn't able to come? Are you here to take me to him?"

"I am."

"Who are you?"

"You're full of questions."

"Is something funny, sir? I don't see the humor in this situation, but you certainly do."

"Pay me no mind, Miss Hart." I should try to remember my manners, but I had been caught off guard.

"You know who I am."

"Yeah, I guess I do."

"Who are you?"

"I'm Grant's younger brother. It's a pleasure to meet you." I held out my hand, but she would not shake it.

"But…where's Mr. Carson?"

Probably in Mrs. Forrester's bed, but…"Er, he's indisposed at the moment. He…couldn't make it." The look on her face—that pretty face, stopped me cold. My smile fell, while I stared at her, as a multitude of emotions passed over her features. "You're not gonna cry, are you?"

"No, sir."

"My mother sent me to fetch you." And that was the God's honest truth, but the next part would be an outright lie. "Grant's been detained on business. He's waiting for you at the ranch."

"We were supposed to be married straight away."

"Is that wise? I mean, why on earth would you marry somebody you never met before?"

"T-that's none of your business." She lifted her chin a notch.

"You don't even know the man!" I had let my irritation show.

"I know plenty. I've been corresponding with him for six months now, maybe longer."

"That's hardly the basis for a relationship. If I were to marry, not sayin' that I'm even thinkin' about something as crazy as that, I'd want to know what I'm gettin' myself into. Who wants to be stuck with a lunatic?"

Her look hardened. "I can assure you, sir, that I'm not a lunatic. I'm perfectly sane."

"All evidence to the contrary, if you don't mind me sayin' so."

"I do mind."

"I'm not the one waitin' for some stranger to show up." She glared at me; her hands had curled into fists. "You wanna hit me, don't you?"

"No, sir. Ladies don't…hit people."

"But you're plenty steamed. I'd be too, actually." *Just wait until you find out my mother deceived you. Poor thing. Poor…pretty little thing.*

An older couple approached, the man carrying a heavy-looking bag. "Well, then," he grinned, "is this Mr. Carson?"

"I am." I tipped my hat. "How do you do?"

"Mr. Aberdeen."

I shook his hand. "Charlie Carson."

"It's the wrong Mr. Carson. This is Grant's younger brother." She glared at me. "Or so he says."

The older woman frowned. "But, where's Grant Carson?"

"Good question," I said, but upon seeing the look of distress on Rebecca's face, I tried to amend my ways. "I've been sent to retrieve, er...Grant's fiancé. I'm sorry he couldn't be here in person to meet you, but...he's in town, I do believe." I pointed at the bag. "I assume that's yours?"

"Yes, sir."

She eyed me with disdain, clearly finding me repugnant. I experienced a moment of doubt, knowing that I wasn't exactly hard on the eyes. Plenty of women had appreciated my company over the years, some even going so far as to say they loved me, although I was hard-pressed to muster those feelings in return. No one had ever hated me at first sight before, but I was clearly not to Miss Hart's liking. Had I been too brash?

"Well, then," said the older woman. "Give me a hug, Rebecca. We're off now."

"You're going to leave me to this...this stranger?"

"You came out here to marry one," I said, interjecting myself into the conversation. I was rewarded with another baleful look. "I'll take the bag, so we can get a wiggle on." I grasped the leather handle, lifting it. "Lordy, what you got in there? Lead bricks?"

"Those are all the things I have in the world, sir."

"Uh-huh." I tossed the bag into the bed of the wagon, resulting in a loud clunk.

"Please be careful!"

"Yep, it sounds like bricks all right."

I turned to face her, expecting that she needed help onto the seat. She was shorter than me by two inches. I wasn't as tall as my brothers, being the runt of the litter. I couldn't help noticing the tininess of her waist, which had been taken in by a corset. Instead of allowing me to help her, she let the old man do the honors, holding onto his arm, as she stepped up.

"If you have any trouble, any trouble at all, you know where to reach us," said Mrs. Aberdeen. "We're here for you, my dear. I'm sorry you didn't meet your fiancé. I'm sure there's a very good reason for his absence."

"There is," I muttered, stepping onto the conveyance and grabbing the reins. "We gotta skedaddle. It'll be nearly dark before we make it home."

"Goodbye," said Rebecca. "I'll write as soon as I can with all the news. I hope you settle nicely with your family. Thank you for accompanying me all this way to…" she glanced around, "the middle of nowhere."

"I do hope this person is who he says he is."

Mrs. Aberdeen's sharp eyes were on me. "I'm reluctant to leave you. It's hardly appropriate to be traveling with a stranger of the opposite sex—alone."

Mr. Aberdeen glanced at me, inquiringly, and I felt compelled to say something. "I'm not in the habit of taking advantage of women. I'm goin' to the Carson Ranch. She's welcome to come with me or stay here. The choice is hers."

"It's not proper, but what can we do?" said Mrs. Aberdeen. "What a muddle."

"Not much," murmured Rebecca. "I'll be fine. I've a perfectly sharp knife at the ready, if Mr. Carson doesn't behave himself."

I whistled through my teeth. "Them are fighting words." I was only teasing, knowing she would find it annoying. I tipped my hat to the older couple. "It was nice meetin' you. You have a good day now."

"Thank you, Mr. Carson." The woman smiled sympathetically at Rebecca. "It'll be fine. I'm sure you're exactly where God intended. Sometimes the path isn't as clear as we would like, but Kansas is meant to be your new home. I'll look for your letters."

"Please say hello to your children for me. I'm sure you're eager to be on your way to see them. I'm sorry I kept you waiting."

"Goodbye, my dear."

As I snapped the reins, Rebecca waved to the couple, while they watched our departure. We trundled through town, passing shops and the saloon, which brimmed with customers, while heading for the open road. I was reluctant to glance in her direction, mostly because I had behaved poorly. I wasn't sure why I had been as rude as I had been. Perhaps, I had taken my irritation out on the poor woman, when it was really my mother I was vexed with.

"There isn't much here," she murmured.

"What were you expectin'?"

"A husband."

"I reckon; you're not ugly by any means. I don't see why you'd have a problem finding a man." I regretted speaking so plainly, but I was rather blunt by nature. "You're prettier than I thought. Really pretty, actually." Did I have to pour it on *that* thickly? I had spoken the truth, knowing that she was possibly the loveliest woman I had ever seen. Would Grant think so too?

"You insult me, and then you compliment me. It's like hot and cold water."

"I'm not...er...all that polite sometimes. I'm sorry."

"Apparently not."

I chose to ignore that. "Where you from again?"

"New York."

"The city?"

"No, Troy."

"Oh. Why'd you want to leave?"

"My mother passed away last year. I was staying with my sister and her husband…but…"

"What?"

"I was the third wheel."

"He was the problem, wasn't he?"

Her head swung in my direction. "Why would you say that?"

"You're awfully easy on the eyes, darlin'. It's not a stretch to imagine he'd try somethin'. He did, didn't he?"

She sat straighter. "I've no intention of discussing this with you."

"Is that why you carry a knife?"

"It's for travel. A woman has to protect herself."

"I'm sorry your ma died."

This had taken her by surprise, as she blinked rapidly. "Thank you."

I didn't want to, but I had begun to feel badly about her situation. She was alone in the world, trapped now in the middle of Kansas without a hope and a prayer. As pretty as she was, I doubted Grant would agree to marry her, or would he?

Four

I had been excited to arrive in Topeka, longing to catch a glimpse of my husband-to-be, but, instead, I had come face-to-face with his younger brother, Charlie. In Grant's last letter, he had stated plainly that we were to be married first thing, as he had made all of the arrangements. Not only was I not married, but I had yet to set eyes on my fiancé. All of my expectations had been dashed, and I was in the company of a loathsome cowboy, who had the manners of an ox.

We stopped to stretch our legs at the midway point, while Charlie disappeared into the prairie on personal business. I lingered near the wagon, scanning the horizon, which ended in a vista of brownish, rolling hills. The wind rustled pretty weeds that looked like sunflowers. Mr. Carson returned, weaving his way through the grass. His shirt was tucked into denim pants, with a thick belt around the middle. He wasn't much taller than I was, long and lean, with a broad set of shoulders. When I had first spoken to him, I had thought he was handsome in a boyish, mischievous sort of way. There was a sparkle in his blue eyes that was appealing, but he ruined the illusion by speaking. As he approached, I felt a plethora of emotions, all of which were confusing.

"You're not gonna cry, are you?" He wasn't smiling now, his look concerned. "I hate it when women cry."

"Something's not right."

"How do you mean?"

"There's something you're not telling me."

He sighed, his shoulders dropping. "I'll leave it up to my ma to explain. This was all her doin' anyway."

"That does not instill me with confidence." What on earth had he meant by that?

He scanned my face, his lips thinning. "You're safe with us, if that's what you're worrying about. We'll take good care of you, till you figure out what you're gonna do."

"Has something happened to Grant? Has he been in an accident? You can tell me. Please tell me."

"He's just fine. He's as healthy as a horse. Now, let's be on our way. The day's almost over. I don't wanna travel in the dark."

"All right."

I had no choice in the matter. I had thrown myself upon the mercy of strangers, and I had made my bed. Charlie's hand was on my waist, lifting me. It lingered for a moment longer than I deemed necessary, and, as I cast a look his way, he lowered his head, hiding his face beneath the brim of the hat. It would be another hour, just as the sun had dipped behind the horizon, before we ambled onto the property; the house in question was larger than I had anticipated. There were several structures: a barn, a smoke house, and what appeared to be a small bunkhouse. There were fences and gates and a field of corn that seemed to stretch out into infinity. The sheer size of the land took my breath away. The wind blew, bringing with it the pungently sweet smell of manure.

A woman in an apron appeared on the front porch, having hurried out at the sound of the wagon. "You brought her!" A broad smile had taken over her face. She was slightly plump, with thick arms and a frilly cap upon her head. "Hello, Rebecca!"

Mr. Carson had come around to my side of the wagon, helping me down, although his hand remained on my forearm longer than necessary. He had now touched me twice, far more than needed, as I could have easily descended myself.

"How was your trip, my dear?" the woman asked, approaching. "Oh, goodness she's pretty. What a doll of a face." Being greeted in such a manner was a surprise, and, as I was taken into her arms, she hugged me fiercely. "Welcome to the Carson Ranch, my dear. I'm so happy to meet you."

"I'm glad to be here, but—"

"I know. Grant wasn't able to meet your train. A...most urgent matter kept him. I'm sure he'll arrive...at any moment." She glanced at her son, her expression bland, but an unspoken communication seemed to pass between them. "Come inside, Rebecca. I've supper on the table. I want to hear all about your travels and everything else you wish to tell me. Grant's going to take one look at you and fall head over heels in love."

Charlie snorted and began coughing. I could not help thinking he was having a laugh at my expense—again. "What's so funny, sir?"

"Not a thing." Mirth gleamed in his eyes. "I'll just grab this eight-hundred pound bag and follow you in."

The house had been built on one floor. The entranceway led into a large parlor, with an enormous stone fireplace. A dog was suddenly underfoot, sniffing me, while wagging a tail vigorously.

"Oh, hello."

"That's Shindy," said Charlie. "You know what shindy means, don't you?"

"No."

"It's a term for confusion and calamity. The first week of havin' him in the house, he chewed on all of our shoes and got into the trash, making a devil of a mess. Then he hid bones in our beds. It was mayhem." He grinned, exposing white, even teeth. "You better watch your things, darlin'. He's a rascal."

The dog, which appeared to be a Golden Retriever, had licked my hand, his nose sniffing me. "I'll keep that in mind. Thank you for the warning." We had passed through the parlor to the kitchen, which was spacious, with a large rectangular table and six chairs.

"What's for supper?" asked Charlie, his hands on his hips.

"Fried chicken with potatoes and gravy. Nothin' special. Do have a seat, Rebecca. You must be starving."

Charlie glanced at me. "Her suppers are legendary. When she says nothin' special, she's lyin'. It's a feast for your mouth, is what it is."

"I've fed the boys already, so it's just us."

"Boys?" I asked.

"Cutter and Derrick are the ranch hands." She had pulled out a chair for me. "Here you go."

No sooner had I situated myself, than a napkin

came my way. Charlie placed it in my lap, his arm brushing mine. "T-thank you."

"You're welcome."

Mrs. Carson approached with a clear pitcher of yellowish fluid, which I assumed was lemonade. "Now then, let's eat. I'm sure you're hungry. You've had such a long journey."

"I am. Thank you." She doled out the chicken and potatoes, filling my plate entirely. "It smells wonderful."

She sat, placing a napkin in her lap. "I do believe this calls for a special prayer, doesn't it, Charlie?"

"If you say so."

"You may say it then, so we can eat."

He bowed his head, murmuring, "Lord, thank you for this fine meal. Thank you for taking care of us and for bringing Miss Rebecca Hart into our lives. She seems like a…nice lady. Please help Grant to hurry his butt up and come home—"

"All right," said Mrs. Carson briskly. "That's enough. Amen."

"Amen," I said, eyeing them with suspicion. "So, why isn't my fiancé here? Mr. Carson was reluctant to talk about it." I caught the look that passed between them, knowing they were hiding something.

"Well," she set her fork down, "there is something you should know. I…had all the best intensions, of course. I…wanted to find a lovely wife for my son. I…know my methods are questionable, but I truly had your happiness and his happiness in mind. My children—God bless them—have grown wild. None seem to want to settle down and have families, and I'm not getting any younger. I…"

"What exactly are you saying?"

"She wrote the letters." Charlie popped a piece of chicken into his mouth, chewing. "It wasn't Grant."

My stomach dropped. "What?"

"You've been romancing my ma." He threw his back, laughing.

I wanted to stab him with my fork, hating that he found this humorous. "I beg your pardon?"

"I'm afraid it's true." Mrs. Carson's look was a mixture of guilt and sympathy. "I did correspond with you, letting you believe I was Grant. I'm sorry, my dear. I was quite desperate to find him a wife. I've given up on my older boys. I thought, perhaps, if Grant were to meet a lovely young woman such as yourself, he would surely marry you."

Charlie's continued laughter grated on my nerves. I had gotten to my feet. "I'm, excuse me." I needed a moment to compose myself, hating that I would cry in front of them. Not knowing where I was going, I hurried down the nearest hallway, finding an empty room to the left, which was darkened. Tears, fast and furious, fell down my cheeks, while I shuddered, knowing that I had made a horrible mistake. Hands grasped my shoulders, and I found myself pressed to a warm, manly chest. "Go away!"

"I'm sorry," Charlie murmured. "I shouldn't laugh at your expense."

"You're a horrible man. Your mother is…horrible too."

"I didn't know about it until this mornin'. She's been scheming for months. It's not your fault, Rebecca. It ain't my fault either."

I didn't want to be this close to him, but it was a comfort feeling his arms around me. He smelled of soap and musk, and, as another wave of tears appeared, I leaned into him, sniffing. "I want to go home."

"Where's that?"

"Anywhere but here. I can't believe I was so deceived. I feel foolish."

"Now, don't say that. You've not met Grant yet. He's in town, somewhere. Once he takes a look at you, he'll make an offer."

"Make an offer?"

"He'll marry you."

"He doesn't even know me. It's your mother who knows me. To think of all the things I told her." I had detailed all my hopes and dreams, believing it was my future husband I was communicating with. "I'm so mortified."

"What kind of secrets did you spill? Is it somethin' scandalous?"

"Nothing I'll tell you, that's for certain."

His lips were near my ear. "What a shame."

I was still in his arms, and I stepped away, eyeing him warily. "I'm fine now."

He reached out, removing a tear from my cheek. "You sure are."

"You're the most impertinent man I've ever met."

"Not really," he chuckled. "You've not been introduced to my older brothers. Wyatt and Bronson are every mother's nightmare."

"Goodness. Now I'm scared."

"You should be."

"I think I'll retire for a while. I need a moment to myself."

"I hope in time, you can forgive my mother. She meant well."

It was odd, but talking to him had been calming. "I don't know. I haven't a clue what I'll do."

"Well, good night then, if I don't see you later."

"Good night. Please tell your mother I said goodnight. Dinner was lovely."

"Sure will, darlin'."

I was given my own room. The bed was covered in a quilt with mis-matched pillows and a knitted blanket. I was in the process of changing into my nightclothes. Mrs. Carson had left a bowl and a pitcher of water, which I used to tidy myself. After I had undone my hair, which hung down my back, I extinguished the lamp and slid beneath the covers.

It was a long time before sleep claimed me, as my mind spun with all the shocking and unpleasant events of the day. I had yet to meet my fiancé, and, when I did, what would I think of him? The memory of how it had felt being in Charlie's arms, his surprising kindness and the gentle manner in which he had held me, played out in my mind, over and over. He was annoying to be sure, but there was something about him that appealed to me.

Five

You have to find Grant," ma said. She had woken me by pushing on my shoulders.

"Aw…go away." I turned on my side, not wanting to look at her.

"Get up, Charlie! You've got to go get your brother. He has to know his fiancé's here."

"He don't want nothin' to do with her. He's in love with that Forrester woman."

"It's a disgrace the way he's carrying on. It has to stop!"

"Even if he got married, he probably won't." That thought left an unpleasant taste in my mouth, thinking of how hurt Rebecca would be, dealing with a faithless husband.

"Please, Charlie. Please go get him. I beg you. He needs to come home."

I tossed the covers back, my feet hitting the

floor. Shindy, who had been sleeping with me, grunted. "Yeah, yeah. I'll do it. Just put the coffee on, all right?"

"Oh, thank you." She hurried from the room.

I stared at the floor, swallowing, trying to dispel the cottony taste in my mouth. "Lord...what a mess." Running fingers through my hair, I sighed, knowing that the morning would be wasted on another silly errand. I had work to do! After I had washed and dressed, I left the house heading for the privy, where after relieving myself, I hurried to the kitchen door. Shindy had followed me out, lifting his leg against a fence post. "Good boy. You keep doing that, and everyone will be happy." Not understanding me, the dog ambled towards the door, entering the kitchen, where he made a beeline for his water bowl.

Ma placed a steaming cup of coffee on the table. "Now, here's the plan. I need you to find Grant and bring him home. You don't have to tell him about Rebecca just yet. Leave that to me. I've something special planned."

"You're scaring me."

"Nonsense. I've got it all figured out."

"Oh, yeah?" Sarcasm laced my tone. "It's gone really well so far." I took a sip of coffee, feeling its heat sliding down my throat. "You make food yet?"

"I'll throw together some flapjacks."

"I hate to be the bearer of bad news, but I don't think Grant's gonna marry that woman. He's not ready to settle down yet with anyone at the moment."

"He needs to come home and get back to work. Cutter and Derrick are planting the northwest field soon, and they'll need help."

"He knows that. I've got my own work to do too. I can't be runnin' around like this. Fences need to be fixed, strays got to be collected, and the books need tending. I'm behind on everything."

"I'll look at the ledgers today."

"Oh, no you don't. I'll not be able to make heads or tails of it, if you mess with the numbers." She was the worst at accounting.

"Fine, but all I ask is that you find your brother. I know you know where he is. You go get him. Then you can fix the fences and things. There's hay that needs to be brought around too."

"I'm well aware of that."

She smiled wistfully. "Thank you, Charlie. You're such a good boy. You're an angel compared to your brothers. I can always count on you." Ma was doing her best to butter me up. I grumbled in reply, taking a long sip of coffee. "You can get moving as soon as you eat." She began mixing the ingredients for the flapjacks, whisking an egg in a porcelain bowl.

I'd had the darnedest time trying to get to sleep

last night, not being able to forget how Miss Hart had felt in my arms. After I had found her crying in the empty bedroom, impulse had taken over, and I had drawn her to me. If I were honest with myself, I'd have to admit that I had been wondering what she would feel like. Ever since my hand had spanned that tiny waist of hers, I'd been slightly obsessed with the thought of holding her. I could still recall the way she smelled, lightly of roses; her breath was sweet as honey…

"Charlie?"

"Huh?"

"You're thinking of something nice."

"No, I'm not."

"Yes, you are. You were smiling."

I sat back in the chair. "Uh, well, yeah. It's a promising day."

"It sure is," she exclaimed brightly. "Now, hurry up and eat, so you can go get that brother of yours."

"Yes, Ma."

This was one chore I did not relish, but I knew exactly where to find Grant, although I hated that I had to bother him in such a manner. He had been gone over a day now, taking advantage of the fact that Mr. Forrester had left on a cattle drive. He would be none too pleased to see me, but I had been given my marching orders, and ma was determined that I retrieve him.

After saddling Sonny, I stepped into the stirrup, tossing a leg over. Cutter and Derrick had taken to the fields, where they would spend most of the day planting and irrigating, while I would miss another hour or two of work. Irritated by this prospect, I urged Sonny into a gallop, cutting across a pasture towards a back road, which led to the town of Elm Hill, where Mrs. May Forrester lived—with her three children. I knew what Grant saw in the comely woman, with her strawberry blonde hair and curvaceous figure, but why he would court her so openly, knowing her husband could return at any moment, boggled the mind. He was asking for a beating or a shooting or worse. When Mr. Forrester found out, he would deal with Grant, and it would not be pretty.

As I rounded the bend, passing the church, I spied the town, seeing several wagons ambling down the road, while children played in the schoolyard, waiting for the teacher to ring the bell. I headed for a back street, Sonny taking my direction well, as I pressed a boot into her flank. Stopping before a clapboard-sided house, I dismounted, tying the horse to a hitching post. I recognized the horse in the nearby pasture. It belonged to Grant.

Not bothering to knock, I found the door unlocked, entering the tidy house, while inhaling the aroma of coffee. "Good morin', sunshine," I proclaimed, striding down a short hallway to the kitchen.

Mrs. Forrester stood before the stove wearing a robe with an apron on. Her hair hung down her back. "Oh, my stars!" A thin, white hand went to her throat.

"Mornin'," I said cheerily, enjoying the look of panic in her eyes, and knowing that my manners were horrendous. "I've come to fetch Grant. Where is he?"

"Don't you know how to knock, Charlie?"

"I do, but why bother? I saw his horse out front. I know he's here."

"He's sleeping."

My grin was lopsided. "I bet."

"You shouldn't enter my house like that. You about gave me a heart attack."

"It's less than what your husband's gonna do when he finds out you've been seeing my brother."

"That's none of your business."

"It's everybody's business. Everybody and their uncle can see his horse in your paddock. You don't think people are that blind and dumb, do you?"

"If you came all this way to lecture me, don't bother." Her look had hardened, which brought out her age, as there were dark circles under her eyes.

"What's this about?" asked a voice from

behind me.

I pivoted on my heel, glancing over my shoulder. "Well, howdy, Grant. Ma's been askin' for you. I've come to take you home." He must have just woken, because his look was bleary-eyed and his hair was a mess.

"I'm leavin' later," he said gruffly. "You didn't need to come here." He approached May, his arms going around her. "That sure smells nice, darlin'. What are you making?"

"Eggs and sausages."

"Hum...I love that," he purred.

This scene of domestic tranquility was enough to turn my stomach. "There've been some changes at the house. It's kinda urgent, Grant. You're needed at home. Believe me, if it wasn't important, I wouldn't be here wastin' my time like this."

"I get that. Why not sit for a spell and have some coffee? We'll ride out together in a bit."

Now, *this* had my attention. "Does that offer come with food? It sure smells nice." My belly growled, even though I just had flapjacks for breakfast. I could always eat again.

"I'll make you a plate," said May.

Mrs. Forrester moved about the kitchen with a certain female grace, and I could see what Grant found appealing, but the fact that she was a married woman cast a rather large question mark upon her character.

"Where are your kids?" I asked.

"Sleeping still. They're too young for school yet." She gave me a look. "I know you think I'm a bad mother and a bad wife."

"I'm not judging you." But that was untrue, because I had been doing just that.

"You never could lie well, Charlie," said Grant. "I know what you're thinkin'."

"Yeah? Well, it's what everyone's thinkin'. You're makin' a fool outta yourself hanging around here. Not only that, but you're gonna get yourself killed by a jealous husband one of these days."

"I doubt Marcus would do that," said May.

"I don't need a lecture from you. I'm a big boy. Let me make my own…decisions." He muttered, "I hate it when people try to tell me what to do."

"I apologize for being a horse's butt."

Grant continued to eat, shrugging. "It's neither here nor there. Forget it."

"Here you are." Mrs. Forrester handed me a plate. "Would you care for more coffee?" She smiled prettily.

"I sure would. Thank you."

"You're welcome."

When we had eaten, and Grant had extracted himself from the clutches of the charming woman, we stood before her house, while a neighbor had taken a bucket of water out, dumping it into a ditch.

"Now what's this all about?" asked Grant. "It must be important. Nobody really cares who I spend my time with. What's happened?"

"Ma's caused all sorts of trouble."

"Oh, for Pete's sake. What now?"

"She's done you a valuable service," I said sarcastically. "She's taken it upon herself to find you a mail order bride."

His mouth fell open. "Pardon?"

"You heard me. She's been corresponding on your behalf with a woman from New York. That woman arrived yesterday, expecting to meet *and* marry you."

"This better be a joke, Charlie. You gotta be pullin' my leg, right?"

"Nope."

He stared at me with a look of incredulity.

I patted him on the back. "Congratulations. You've got yourself a pretty little fiancé waitin' for you. She's a sweet thing, but she does have a bit of a mouth on her."

"If this is your idea of fun, brother, you'd better tread carefully." There was a hint of steel in his voice. "I've no intention of marrying anyone, least of all a stranger."

"I know that. I didn't have anything to do with the woman coming out here. I knew nothin' about it until yesterday. You'll have to take up your grievances with ma. She's the mastermind behind this…farce." I placed a booted foot into the stirrup. "Yep, it's turning out to be a hell of a day, if I do say so myself."

Six

I had worn a striped yellow dress, with a fitted bodice. Having arranged my hair in a braided bun, I examined myself in the mirror, hoping that I looked appealing enough for my husband-to-be. Mrs. Carson was all smiles when I appeared in the kitchen.

"Hello, Rebecca. Don't you look lovely."

"Thank you." Shindy ambled over, rubbing himself against my leg. "Good morning, dog." I bent to pet him, and he licked my hand. "You're very friendly."

"Have a seat. I've some coddled eggs ready with bacon. Do you drink tea or coffee?"

"I prefer tea."

"With milk and sugar?"

"That sounds lovely."

She placed these items on the table. "Yesterday

must've come as a shock to you. I'm sorry about that. You probably think poorly of me now."

"Because of the letters?"

"Yes, of course, and for lying to you." She set a plate of food before me.

"Thank you."

Then she took a seat at the other end of the table; her look was earnest. "I should explain myself. It's the least I could do. I've had a hard time raising four boys, Rebecca. My oldest sons went and fought in the war, but they came back wild. I don't know what they've done or seen, because they won't talk about it, but it affected them badly. I've pretty much given up on them. There are rumors that Bronson is an outlaw, but I don't want to believe that. Then there's Grant, who I had such high hopes for. He was a smart child, always the first to finish his schoolwork and help with the chores. He had potential, but I think Wyatt and Bronson's influence rubbed off a bit, because he's gone astray."

"And this is the sort of environment you would send an innocent woman into?" I hated that I sounded peeved, but I was!

"I know." She hung her head. "It was a horrible thing to do, but you said you had no one. Your folks are all passed on now, and you didn't want to stay with your sister. I thought I'd be doing you a favor finding you a new home."

"With a pack of outlaws."

"Oh, now, no." She looked offended. "We've a real working farm here. I don't deal in underhanded businesses, well, not often. Whatever Wyatt and Bronson are up to, I've no knowledge of it. I see them occasionally when they come by, but that's all. They wouldn't tell me what they're doing anyhow."

"I'm sorry. That was harsh."

"I understand your anger. I deserve it, because I've deceived you outright. I've taken advantage of you. I just hope you don't leave, Rebecca. You and Grant would make a darling couple. You're such a pretty girl. I had no idea you were so pretty. The drawing doesn't do you justice at all."

That had been rather heartfelt and sweet. "Thank you."

"Oh! I hear them now." She got to her feet. "Excuse me for a moment."

She raced out of the room, while I ate the eggs, wiping my mouth with a napkin. The sounds of voices registered in the hallway.

"What in tarnation is goin' on here?" asked an angry man. "I've been told you've procured a wife for me? Are you outta your mind?"

"Now calm down, Grant. I know you're angrier than a hornet, but what I've done is for your own good."

I had gotten to my feet, bracing myself for a

"Here she is," he said happily, approaching. His hands were on my shoulders, as he brought me forward. "Here's the lovely Rebecca Hart. Isn't she pretty as a peach?"

Goodness, he was irritating, having done that on purpose, showing me off like a prize cow at the fair. I glared at him over my shoulder.

"That she is." Grant extended a hand. "It's good to meet you. Welcome to the Carson Ranch. I'm Grant Carson."

"Rebecca Hart. I'm happy to make your acquaintance." His grip was firm. Charlie had yet to release me, his fingers clawing possessively at my shoulders.

This was not lost on Grant. "You can quit pawing Rebecca at any time."

"So sorry."

I glanced over my shoulder, meeting his gaze, which sent the strangest sensation into the pit of my stomach. It wasn't unpleasant in the least, but it was confusing.

"Well, then," said Mrs. Carson. "Why don't we sit in the parlor and get to know one another better."

"I've things to do," said Charlie. "You'll have

to excuse me. Somebody's gotta work around here." He strode down the hallway, his boots clicking on the wooden floor.

Grant was tall, dark, and handsome, but there was an edge to his look, which hinted of danger. I could sense his frenetic energy, which was entirely different from my own. He reminded me a little of a wolf that had been trapped in a cage.

In the parlor, I sat on a blue velvet sofa, while Mrs. Carson took the rocking chair. Grant remained standing before the fireplace with his hand on the mantel, his gaze darting between us.

"I have a confession to make," said Maggie. "I've been writing letters to Rebecca in your stead. I'm sorry about that; I really am. She's agreed to marry you, Grant. She came all the way from New York to start a new life."

"And what exactly do you expect me to do about it?"

"Well, marry the girl."

"Just like that, eh?"

"Why not? You're nearly twenty-six, son, and it's time to start thinking about a family and a farm of your own. You've sowed your oats long enough."

"And you're gonna be the one to decide that for me?"

I watched carefully, as a little tick jumped in his cheek. Oh, dear. He was incredibly angry. I didn't know what to say, but I had to do something. "It's fine." They glanced at me. "I'll work out another set of tickets and go home. I've made a dreadful mistake."

"You can't do that!" Mrs. Carson got to her feet. "You only just arrived here. You haven't even spoken to Grant. Once you two have a conversation, I'm sure you'll find common ground."

I had been put in the most impossible situation, feeling horribly out of place. "Please, don't worry about me. I'll be fine."

"Would you give us a moment?" Grant looked like he wanted to strangle the woman.

"I will."

Getting to my feet, I was suddenly eager to be away from them, feeling stuck in the middle of a family squabble that had nothing to do with me. In the hallway, I continued, until I found the door, leaving the house. The air was fresher today than last night, the aroma of manure having diminished. Strolling towards the barn, I took a moment to have a look around, impressed by the neat rows of fences that held horses and the cows in the distance that grazed freely.

"That was fast," said a voice behind me.

I turned, observing Charlie, who held a bucket. "They're talking."

"I bet."

His grin was slightly obnoxious. "You're taking far too much pleasure in this."

"I am. It's the craziest thing that's happened in a long while. I can't wait to see how it plays out."

Glory be, he was irritating. I glanced at the bucket. "What are you doing?"

"Feedin' the chickens before I head out."

"Chickens? Might I watch?"

"Certainly."

I followed him around the barn to a large henhouse, which held a variety of chickens, including babies. "Oh, how adorable." He tossed the contents of the bucket inside, as they raced to the far corner of the enclosure, screeching with fear. "They don't seem to like humans much."

"Nope. Catchin' 'em is a chore."

Something moved at my feet. Shindy had found us. "Hello." I petted his head, as his mouth opened slightly, revealing a darkly colored tongue. "What am I going to do?" I had uttered this out loud, mostly to myself.

"About what?"

"This predicament."

"I thought you'd catch the next train." He approached with the bucket. "You don't want to stay here, do you?"

I met his gaze. "I was promised a husband."

"Eh, they're not all they're cracked up to be." His grin was teasing.

"You laugh at my troubles. It's rude."

"I'm just tryin' to make light outta a bad situation, is all."

"It's not helpful."

"Have you spoken to Grant?"

"No."

"Why don't you wait till you have a talk. He might just be crazy enough to marry you. You never know." He had gone from teasing to insulting, which I had come to expect from him.

"I suppose." The little experience I'd had with men wasn't helpful at all in that heady, confounding moment. As we stared into each other's eyes, the air crackled with a pleasing, vibrant energy. What was this? An overwhelming compulsion to kiss him had me swaying in his direction.

"There you are," said a voice behind me.

"Ah, saved in the nick of time." Charlie grinned. "Your fiancé is a charming woman, brother. You'd best stake your claim before I steal her for myself."

"Yeah, you'd say that." He came to stand beside me. "I'm sorry I've been so rude. I hope we can start again." He held out his hand. "Grant Carson. Happy to make your acquaintance."

"Rebecca Hart." I shook his hand, but all I could think about were Charlie's words. *You'd best stake your claim before I steal her for myself…*

"Let's take a walk, shall we?" He smiled politely. "Then maybe we can figure somethin' out that'll work for both of us."

"I'd like that." I smiled also, feeling that things were finally heading towards a solution, although I was slightly baffled about the things Charlie had said. Perhaps, he was a hopeless flirt, and everything out of his mouth was a tease.

As we began for the road, I glanced over my shoulder. Charlie, who stood by the barn door, wasn't smiling anymore.

Seven

I had taken a ridiculous amount of pleasure in watching my brother squirm this morning, but...after Rebecca strolled off with him, something had changed. I would never admit it to anyone, not even God, but I enjoyed being in her company, and I looked forward to seeing her.

As she started down the road with Grant, I stared after them for the longest time, which added to my irritation. I needed to ride the fences and round up strays, but here I was, pining for a woman. Could that be so? Shaking myself from these unwanted feelings, I headed for the paddock to retrieve Sonny. I had wasted enough time as it was. I had work to do.

There was a fair amount of space and peace being out on our land; the two hundred acres we owned were filled with tall grass, which the animals fed on. We were expecting a shipment of cattle from Texas next week, adding to the hundred or so we already had. Times were prosperous, but it took a great deal of work to assure things ran smoothly. Being the more responsible of my brothers, I had stayed with my mother to manage the ranch. Wyatt and Bronson were too busy giving in to their vices to care about such things, and Grant had been led astray by a married woman, who had cheating on her mind.

I found my brother alone later that day, sitting on a rocking chair on the front porch. He held a glass filled with what looked like whiskey. "How goes it?"

"It's going."

"What have you decided about Rebecca?"

He shrugged. "I should kill that woman."

"Rebecca?"

"No, ma. Did you know she wrote poetry in those letters? Poetry that supposedly came from me!" He shook his head. "Of all the crazy things I've heard. That takes the prize."

I sat next to him, gazing at the mud caked to my boots. I'd have to brush that off before I went inside. "So, are you gonna marry her?"

"I guess."

I should have known he would say that. "You...find her attractive?"

"She's handsome enough." He lifted the glass, taking a sip. "But I don't plan on givin' up May."

"I see. You think it's all right to have a wife and then carry on with a married woman?"

"Don't give me that!" Anger laced his tone. "I didn't ask for this! I'm not keen on settlin' down now. I still got…some hay to make before I commit to a woman."

"Then you shouldn't marry her."

"Somebody has to!" He glanced at me. "You were pawing all over her. Why don't you make her an offer?"

"Because she came here for you."

"Bah! Bull pony!" He finished the drink, grimacing. "What a mess."

"Did you set a wedding date?"

"Yeah," he murmured sourly. "I guess."

"Looks like it's as good as settled."

"I'm as good as cooked."

"You'll do fine," I laughed. "All you gotta do is stand at the end of the aisle, and she'll meet you there."

"I'm not thinkin' about that right now."

"When's the wedding?"

"Saturday."

I whistled through my teeth. "You got till the weekend then." Grant belched loudly in response. "It's time you make an honest woman…out of someone. You weren't thinkin' of marrying May, were you?"

"I've got real feelings for her. It's not just…the

time we spend in bed, but that's awfully good too." He grinned crookedly.

"Her husband's due home any day. He'll tan your hide when he finds out you've been seein' his wife."

"I'm aware of that."

"I really wish you'd give Rebecca a chance and not bring May into your marriage. I'd say, finish it with that woman. No good will come from it."

He got to his feet. "I'm headin' out."

"Where are you going?"

"I don't know, but I'm tired of being lectured. Tell Rebecca I said goodbye."

"When can she expect to see you again?"

"I'll be back in the mornin'. I got things to do in town. Will you do me a favor?"

"What?"

"There's a social tonight. Will you take Rebecca and show her a good time?"

"You're not serious."

"I am. She needs a distraction."

"Why don't *you* take her? That'll give you the chance to get to know her better."

"I gotta talk to May. I gotta break the news to her. She's liable to scratch my eyes out when she hears I have a fiancé. She has a bit of a temper on her."

"She's got no right, seein' she has a husband."

His expression hardened. "I'm weary of this

conversation. I'll be back in the mornin'.'"

He stalked towards his horse, while I sat staring after him. For some reason, the prospect of taking Rebecca to a social didn't bother me in the least. I would have to bring ma along, which was the proper thing to do, as we needed a chaperone. If my brother refused to entertain our lovely houseguest, then why couldn't I? The thought existed that I might even steal a kiss or two. I wasn't fond of dancing, but holding her in my arms appealed greatly. With renewed enthusiasm, I got to my feet. It was time I took matters into my own hands.

Waiting for women to get ready was always tedious. I nursed a whiskey on the front porch, while Rebecca and ma prettied themselves up, fixing hair and dabbing on rose water. They had readily agreed to the outing, mostly because ma looked forward to introducing Grant's fiancé to all and sundry. By the time they emerged from the house, my belly was full of liquor, while a heady warmth spread through me. Rebecca wore the dress she had on earlier, but she had gussied it up with a knitted shawl.

"Sorry we kept you waiting," she said, smiling brightly. After Grant had agreed to marry her, she'd had a rather dramatic change in personality, as her smiles came more readily. That magnetic beam was now fixed on me.

"All right then. Let's go have us a grand ol' time." I helped her into the wagon, extracting a great deal of pleasure from touching her arm. I had arranged it so she would sit next to me, with ma on the end. When I took my seat, I leaned towards her, catching her scent, which was infused with floral undertones. "Hang on. If you fall off, I ain't gettin' you."

"No one's falling off," said ma. "It's unfortunate Grant's not here tonight. He really should be with us."

"We'll have a fine time without him," I murmured under my breath. Feeling eyes on me, I turned to Rebecca, who smiled shyly. "You comfortable, honey?"

"Yes, I am."

"You look comfortable."

"Oh, quit lollygagging, and let's get on with it."

I pulled on the reins. "Yes, Ma."

A short while later, lights appeared in the distance, the inhabitants of Elm Hill having settled and built houses in a swath of land bordered by two distinct streams. The line of trees on each side, the cottonwoods and willows, acted as a barrier to the wind when things became blustery during storms. The social was held at the town hall, which was situated midway down Main Street. There were wagons and carriages out front, with accompanying horses affixed to hitching posts.

"This will give you the opportunity to meet all the folks in town," said May happily. "I'm mighty proud to introduce you as my future daughter-in-law."

I glanced at Rebecca to gauge her reaction, and predictably, a huge smile lit her face. She was happier than I had ever seen her; her dreams of marriage were about to come true. A prick of annoyance registered, as these thoughts were bothersome. My brother was about to marry a good and kind woman, while continuing to cavort around like a bachelor. That sat ill with me, indeed.

Helping the ladies to alight, I gripped Rebecca's arm, not releasing it for a good minute after her feet were firmly on the ground. Not only that, but I continued to hold onto her, leading her into the building, which brimmed with folks laughing and talking, while musicians played in the far corner. I wasn't fond of socials, hating to dance, but I would avail myself of liquor all the same. I wouldn't mind waltzing with Miss Hart later either, after I had fortified myself with enough whiskey.

Ma led Rebecca around the room, introducing her to nearly every person in town, which included the judge, John Parker, Doc Winston, and Pastor John, as well as other business owners. I stood by the refreshment table, watching their reactions to her. Ma preened under the attention, clearly relishing the fact that one of her boys had finally agreed to marry.

"Well, hello there, Charlie," said a voice from behind me. "What brings you to town? I don't believe I've ever seen you at a social."

I turned to find Vivian Hendricks, a woman I had known since childhood. "I'm the driver."

"I beg your pardon?" Her features were handsome, to be sure, but I had never been tempted to court her.

"I brought my ma and our houseguest."

"I met her. She's marrying Grant?"

"Yes, she is."

She grinned. "How'd y'all pull off that miracle? From what I heard, he's sweet on a certain married woman."

"Er," I removed the hat, scratching my head, "that's an unsubstantiated rumor, Vivian." Her laugher filled my ears.

"Right." She glanced over her shoulder, at Miss Hart. "She's a comely woman. I feel sorry for her, though. It's a shame she's being misled. She'll beat him with a broom after the wedding, when she finds out he's faithless."

Not liking the direction of the conversation, I said curtly, "I gotta go and dance. Excuse me."

"Have a wonderful time." Sarcasm dripped from her voice. "But come dance with me later. I might be married…but you were always my second choice."

Stunned by this announcement, I pivoted on my heel. "What?"

"You Carson boys sure can turn a girl's head, but you're as wild as prairie grass. Heaven help any woman who falls in love with you. It'll lead to nothin' but heartache."

I advanced on her, and she backed up a step or two. "I ain't like my brothers, Vivian. If I were in love with a woman, I'd never hurt her. I'd love and cherish her forever. She'd never have to wonder where I am or who I'm with. She'd be the only one I'd want."

Her eyes widened. "My goodness. Perhaps I've made a mistake. Maybe you should've been first on my list."

Eight

The talk I had with Grant had put my mind at ease. We had taken a walk, which had allowed us to speak privately, and he had agreed to marry me. He'd said, "We've both been duped by my ma. I had no idea she was writing letters back east, for a mail order bride."

"I didn't know either."

"I feel pretty darn awful that you had to come all this way to find out you've been deceived."

"She meant well."

"Look," he'd stopped walking, "I've been thinkin' about the circumstance we're in, and…I should step up and take care of the matter."

"You don't have to. I've already made up my mind to go home. I don't want to be a burden on anyone. I…just have to get some money together for the train fare."

"That won't be necessary. I'll…er…marry

you."

Shock left me nearly speechless. "You will?"

He nodded, although he looked slightly distressed. "Yes, ma'am."

"Why would you do that?"

"To save your reputation and to make my ma happy."

"Those are horrible reasons to marry."

"You came out here expectin' to get hitched to a total stranger. Isn't that just as bad?"

"I thought I knew you. We talked about everything in those letters."

His look was grim. "Yeah, well, you got the fantasy ma created. I'm a different person."

"I know. That's why I'm leaving. You don't have to marry me out of obligation."

He stared at his feet, kicking a stone. "Why don't we take the week to get to know each other? Let's plan the weddin' on Saturday, and if we change our mind, we'll just…er…send you back east."

Now I was confused. "We'll set a date, but it might not happen?"

"Oh, tarnation! I'll marry you either way. I don't really want to talk about this anymore. What's done; is done."

"Are you certain? You don't seem happy about it in the least."

"You're a good lookin' woman. I'd have no

complaints about being married to you...I'm just...sorta set in my ways. I...like a drink every now and then and...er...oh, never mind."

"I won't hinder your lifestyle, Grant. I'll try to be as unobtrusive as possible. Maybe one day...we might develop feelings for each other? Do...do you want children?"

His hands slid into his pockets, while he gazed into the distance. "Uh, yeah. Ma's been wantin' grandbabies."

"Do *you* want them?"

"I do...some day."

That was as good of an answer as I was going to get from him. He was reluctant to commit to me, and I couldn't blame him. We had set a date to be married, but I knew there was a chance he might change his mind. If I failed to marry by Saturday, then I knew what I would do. I would pack my bag and go home—wherever that was.

These musings occupied my mind, while I nursed a glass of lemonade, staring across the room where Charlie stood near the refreshment table talking to a woman. He had not danced yet, preferring to remain in the background. I had to wonder who the woman was, but the gleam on her left hand revealed a wedding band. The Carson's knew everyone in Elm Hill, as I had been introduced to many people tonight. My only concern at the moment was a strange one, as I was worried he would dance with her. Why this thought plagued me was peculiar. He had been kind enough to drive us to town, and it was silly of me to want to dance with him, but I did.

After the Virginia reel had ended, the musicians began to play something softer, and couples took to the floor to waltz. It was then that Charlie strode towards me. His expression was nearly unreadable, but my pulse began to quicken with the hope that he would ask me to dance.

"How's the lemonade?"

"That's what you came over to ask me?" My heart sank.

His eyes drifted over my face. "I suppose."

"It's fine." He seemed entirely ill at ease. "How's your drink?"

"Potent."

"Well, they make whiskey that way, I suppose."

"I'm…not much of a dancer."

"There's nothing to the waltz. It's simple enough." To my chagrin, he took the glass out of my hand, placing it on nearby table. "What are you doing?"

"Let's cut a rug then, eh?" He took my hand, leading me towards the dance floor.

"Ouf! Your manners are abominable; they truly are." I was in his arms, held tightly, while he clasped my right hand, swinging me in a circle. We glided about the room, while the music played.

"You're better than I thought."

"Pardon?" He glanced at me.

"You dance just fine."

"Thank you." We were nearly the same height, with perhaps a two-inch difference, and it seemed we fit together perfectly. His grip around my waist was snug, while he clutched my hand.

"I guess you're gonna get your weddin' after all, huh?"

"It seems that way."

"Congratulations."

"That's kind of you."

"Looks like your trip out here wasn't in vain."

"Well, hopefully not." He met my gaze, his look questioning. "I mean, I hope it all goes well. Grant seems rather reluctant. I hate to think I'm forcing someone to commit to me…for life."

"Uh-huh."

"You're a man of few words tonight," I giggled. It seemed as if his grip tightened further. "Your dancing skills are better than average. Do you attend many socials?"

"Absolutely not."

"Why?"

"It's not my idea of a relaxing evenin'. I'm doin' you and ma a favor. That's all."

"Well, thank you for everything. I'm having a marvelous time." His look was slightly sour, and I could not help wondering what had put him in such a foul mood.

He said little after that, and, once the waltz had ended, we went our separate ways. I was on my feet for the rest of the evening, partaking in the Patty Cake Polka, the Carolina Promenade, and several quadrilles. By the end of the night, I was exhausted. Mrs. Carson and I chatted happily on the drive back, while Charlie appeared stone-faced and his posture stiff. After we had pulled into the dusty drive of the ranch, he helped me from the wagon.

"Thank you again for taking us to town." He mumbled something under his breath, which left me entirely flummoxed.

Wanting to free myself of the corset and change into something comfortable, I hurried to my room, where I discovered Shindy curled up on the bed. "Oh, you! What are you doing in here?" The dog took up a fair amount of the mattress; his long legs were crossed before him. "You shouldn't be in here."

I hated to move him, as he looked content. Instead, I made quick work of changing, tossing a white nightgown over my head. Then I freed my hair, releasing the tangles with a brush. I had Shindy's undivided attention, the dog sniffing in my direction. When I was ready for bed, I eyed him dubiously.

"You can't sleep here." He had not moved an

inch. "Come on now." I gently prodded him, shoving him from the rear. "Off you go." Big black, glossy eyes stared at me. "I can't sleep with you in my bed, you silly animal." Again I gave him a shove, but he refused to budge. Sliding from the bed, I opened the door. "Out you go! Come on, boy. Shindy! Shindy! Go, boy, go!"

"You stole my dog."

Charlie glared at me. "I did not. I found him in my room. You're more than welcome to take him. He's not listening to me."

"He looks comfortable."

"I'm sure, but there's nowhere for me to sleep."

"You little traitor," he murmured. He whistled between his teeth, and the dog jumped to his feet, bounding to the floor. "There you go. Git on outta here."

I met Charlie's gaze. "Thank you."

"What else you plan on stealing around here?"

"What?"

"My dog prefers you."

"I'm friendlier than you are right now. You've been in a foul mood all night. Was it something I said?"

"Nope."

"I'm sorry you didn't enjoy yourself. You're not a bad dancer." He grunted in reply. "Maybe it was the whiskey."

"I didn't have enough, actually."

"Well, thank you for removing your dog. He was really reluctant to go."

"He sleeps with me."

"Is there room in the bed?" I laughed. "He's not a small animal."

"We sorta…bunch up together. I used to take him with me in my cattle drive days. He slept on my bedroll and kept me nice and warm."

"I see."

His gaze slid across my face. "You sure enjoyed yourself tonight. Is there anyone you didn't dance with?"

Was he jealous? "My card was full, wasn't it?" There was something adorable about his expression. When he grinned, he looked like an impish little boy. I had a marvelous time dancing, and my spirits were still soaring. Impulse took over, and I leaned in, hugging him. "Thank you again."

He stiffened slightly, mostly because I had stunned him, but he was quick to grasp me, holding me tightly. My face rested in the crook of his neck, while the aroma of citrus and sandalwood, with a hint of whiskey filled my senses. I pulled away, as the embrace had gone on for far too long. It never should have occurred in the first place.

"Well," I said somewhat breathlessly. "I'd best

go to bed." His look was inscrutable, but those pale blues eyes remained focused on me. "Good night, Charlie."

"Good night, Rebecca."

With great reluctance, I shut the door, leaning against it. It was several minutes before my heart slowed to a normal pace.

Nine

Rebecca was right. I was in a sour mood, but I couldn't quite put my finger on why. Since Grant had agreed to marry her, she seemed to blossom, her cheeks were rosier than ever, her smile had transformed her face, and she was softer, lovelier than before. I wasn't the only one who noticed this, as men had flocked around her, asking her to dance. She was engaged in this manner the entire night, while I sipped whiskey and stewed by the sidelines.

Then she had hugged me…

It was a struggle to sleep, tossing and turning, upsetting Shindy, who jumped to the floor and slept on my trousers and shirt. I wasn't much for picking up after myself, and my room was typically a mess. In the morning, I threw water on my face and brushed my teeth, while eyeing my tired-looking features in a mirror. The aroma of coffee had me reaching for the door, which I opened, nearly colliding with Rebecca.

"Oh! You scared me!" She had on a blue calico dress with a white collar and long sleeves. "You slept in." Shindy darted from the room, but he stopped to sniff her skirts, rubbing against her leg. She bent to pet him. "Hello, boy."

"I've ledgers to go over," I grumbled.

"What sorts of ledgers?"

"Arithmetic." I hated numbers. Memories of the schoolroom assailed me. I'd had my knuckles smacked with a ruler on many occasions, because I struggled to add and subtract correctly. "Nothin' for you to worry about." I hated that I sounded so cross, but I'd slept badly, images of Rebecca floating through my mind, although she was naked in all of them. I had woken in a most uncomfortable state; every nerve ending in my body was wound tighter than a bale of hay. I'd have to go to town later to…find some relief, but it would only reduce the flames, leaving the bonfire raging.

"Well, I was rather good at arithmetic in school. I could have a look at it, if you want."

"Women and counting don't mix."

"I beg your pardon?"

"Pa said women and numbers are like oil and water."

Her hands went to her hips. "That's a silly thing to say."

"Are you callin' my pa silly?"

"It's just not true. A woman is as adept as a man when it comes to numbers."

"Not from what I heard."

"Oh, for gracious sake, Charlie. Must we argue this early in the morning? You look terrible. What happened to you?"

I had wicked fantasies about you all night long, you irritating little minx. "Nothin'. Nothing's wrong."

"Can't we call a truce?" Her hand was on my arm. "I'm excellent at sums, sir. You should let me look at the books. It's the one thing I can do to help around here. I feel utterly useless. Mrs. Carson does all the cooking and cleaning, and I…sit and stare at the walls. I do wish to be helpful."

Then take that dress off and… "All right." I had to stop thinking like this.

"You'll let me help?"

"I suppose so. You seem determined to do it. I need coffee. Have you had breakfast yet?"

"I have."

"I must've slept in." It was later than I thought.

"Good morning," said ma, who appeared at the end of the hallway. "Well, come on. I've been waiting for you. Breakfast is ready." She was in a chirpy, happy mood.

"Good mornin'." We followed her into the kitchen.

"Did the dog sleep with you?" asked Rebecca.

"No, he didn't. I hogged the bed."

"Grant will be by soon. He needs to repair that hole in the barn, and then he's taking me to town." She removed a kettle from the stove.

Rebecca's smile grew. "Oh, how wonderful. I can't wait to see him." She glanced at me. "Isn't that good news?"

I had taken a seat, eyeing a basket of freshly baked bread on the table. "Oh, yeah. Just…marvelous." I needed coffee to quell the beginning of a rather large headache. I reached for the metal pot.

"You should come along, Rebecca, when we go to town. Have you chosen your wedding dress yet?"

"I brought one."

"That was thoughtful of you."

"I should hang it up. It might need pressing."

"I'd love to see it. I've an old veil you may use, if you want."

"How kind. I was lacking a veil."

They prattled on about the wedding, while I sat listening, my scowl deepening. I could not remember the last time I had been in such a foul mood. I prayed it went away by lunchtime. After breakfast, I sat in pa's old study going over the books, which were leather-bound ledgers filled with columns of numbers. After the first page, my headache worsened, and I sat miserably, holding my forehead in my hands.

"I'm sorry to bother you." Rebecca stood in the doorway.

"I'm workin'. What is it?" She approached, coming in behind me, which I found odd. I turned to gaze at her.

"I can add those, if you want."

"I was doin' just fine."

Pointing to the fourth line down, she said, "You missed here. This is four-twenty-five, not four-eighty."

I snapped the ledger shut, glaring at her. "If I wanted help, I'd have asked for it."

"Must you be so bad-tempered? Your eyes are red, and you look dreadfully tired. Maybe you should return to bed."

Anger propelled me to my feet, while I tried my best to tower over her, although I was only about two inches taller. "Now, listen here. I don't appreciate you sticking your nose in my business. Why don't you help ma in the kitchen or somethin'."

"I could help you." She didn't seem frightened of me at all. "I need something to do before Grant arrives. Your mother already cleaned the kitchen. I'd only be underfoot there. Must you be so stubborn, Charlie? You clearly loathe accounting, and I'm quite good at it."

She did have a point, but I would never admit it. We weren't more than a foot apart, and I leaned in, inhaling her sweet fragrance. I was a hairsbreadth away from kissing her, when ma's voice cut through my consciousness like the rusty creak of a barn door.

"Charlie!"

"If you love numbers so much, have at it," I said.

"Thank you."

Ma appeared in the doorway. "I need firewood, son, and there's none. I won't be able to make lunch without it."

That was a chore and a half. "Fine. I'll do it."

Rebecca had taken a seat at the desk, glancing at the ledger.

"Is she going over the numbers?"

"Yes, I am."

"I'm givin' her a trial run. If everything's all muddled up afterwards, she's fired." My humor had returned, which was a relief. If only the headache would go away.

Rebecca grinned. "That won't happen. I'm quite good at this, but from the looks of it, I'll have to go back several pages and fix things." She began flipping through the book.

"Thank you, my dear," said ma. "We needed

someone to straighten everything out. It's been months since it's been done."

Rebecca glanced at me. "Are there receipts anywhere?"

"Top right drawer."

"Thank you."

The wood would not chop itself, so I left the house, heading for the barn. There was nothing like manual labor to take one's mind off things, and, as I began to split logs, I let my thoughts wander, although after ten minutes, I slammed the ax down, embedding it in a stump.

"Can I not think about her for five minutes?" I grumbled, angered with myself. "Five minutes?" Rolling up my sleeves, I attacked a new log, splitting it with one swipe, the pieces falling to the ground. A motion in the distance caught my eye, as I spied Grant's horse heading this way. Leaving the ax in a piece of wood, I approached my brother, who dismounted before the house.

"So, you've finally returned to get some work done, eh?"

"Yeah."

"Are you still gonna marry Rebecca?"

An eyebrow lifted. "You seem awfully interested in her."

"Just want to know."

"I said I would, so I am."

"Did you tell May?"

"Yeah."

That wasn't the answer I had been expecting. "What's she think about your upcoming nuptials?"

"None of your business." He'd removed the saddle, tossing it over a fence.

"She took it that well, huh?"

He gave me a look, before leading the horse to the pasture. "Not really."

"But you still plan on marrying her?"

"Give it a rest," he muttered cantankerously. "I don't really want to talk about it. I got a pile of things to do."

Why was it that I had been hoping he had changed his mind? "All right, brother. Whatever you say."

Ten

I worked on the ledgers for over two hours, making corrections. Whoever had calculated the debits and credits had gotten nearly every line wrong. By the time I had straightened it all out, there was a surplus of over four hundred dollars. It had originally showed a loss of over a thousand. That was quite a difference.

Grant would be driving us to town today, which overjoyed me. I longed to spend more time with my fiancé in the hopes of getting to know him better, although he did not seem as enthusiastic. I was seated next to him with Mrs. Carson on the end, but he failed to look at me even once, preferring to gaze straight ahead.

He did ask, "So, how was the social last night? Did you enjoy yourself, Rebecca?"

"She danced with nearly every bachelor in town," said Maggie.

"I did not."

"You didn't sit once after you waltzed with Charlie. Every man in the room wanted to be your partner."

"That's a gross exaggeration."

"I'm sorry I missed it," said Grant. "I…had other plans."

"Now that you'll be married, you needn't bend an elbow at the bar every night of the week," said Maggie. "It's time to settle down and make babies."

This announcement brought a hint of color to my cheeks. "Oh, I'm sure we won't have to rush into anything."

"I've been waiting a long time for grandbabies. I certainly won't hold my breath for Wyatt and Bronson to marry anytime soon. I blame myself for their upbringing. I should've been stricter with them, but after they left for the war," she gazed at her hands, "they weren't the same again."

"The war was hard on everyone," I said. "You mustn't take all the blame upon yourself, Mrs. Carson."

"My boys fought admirably in Tennessee and Virginia. Wyatt was at the Battle of Bristoe Station, but he refuses to talk about it."

"I can imagine." We were nearly in town now; the thoroughfare bustled with wagons and people. "My goodness, what a crush."

"The mail comes on Thursday," said Grant.

"We should stop by the post office," said Maggie. "I might have a letter. Wyatt and Bronson write occasionally."

"I'll drop you ladies off in the center then. I've got to visit the barbershop. I'll fetch you in an hour." He politely helped us from the wagon, although his touch on my person was brief.

"Thank you, Grant," I said.

He smiled courteously. "You're welcome."

I accompanied Mrs. Carson to the post office, where she had a letter waiting, although it was not from one of her boys. It was a business correspondence. Then we strolled down the boardwalk, entering the mercantile, perusing the ready-made dresses. I had found the miscellaneous bin, and I proceeded to gather scraps of cloth.

There were several women in the store and more at the counter, having their purchases bundled. When I had chosen the items I wanted, I approached the salesclerk. The woman in front of me had just paid for her things, and after securing her billfold; she turned to look at me.

"Excuse me."

"I'm sorry," I said.

She moved to pass, eyeing Mrs. Carson, who was examining cookware at a nearby table. Then something changed in her countenance, as her pleasant expression fell. "I've not seen you before."

"Pardon?"

"Are you staying at the Carson Ranch?"

"I am."

Understanding shone in her eyes. "Oh, I see. You must be Rebecca Hart."

"I am."

"I'm May Forrester." She drew me aside, and the woman who had been waiting behind us approached the counter. "I do believe you're about to marry my lover." She had lowered her voice.

I gasped, shocked, not knowing what to say. "I...beg your pardon?"

"He told me all about it."

"I'm sorry, but you've completely lost me."

"He won't tell you the truth, but I will. I love him, you hear? I love that man. I'd do anything for him. I'm leavin' my husband for him."

Stunned, I could only stare at her. "A-are you speaking about Grant Carson?"

"I am. He's *my* man. He'll never marry you. He loves me!"

People were now staring, and the situation was mortifying. "I...excuse me." I dropped the items I had been about to purchase on a nearby table, hastening for the door.

Mrs. Carson took one look at who I had been speaking to and followed me out. "Don't listen to that horrible woman!" She hurried down the boardwalk to catch up. "She's a disrespectable wretch, that one. All she does is stir up trouble."

"Did you hear what she said?" I glanced over her shoulder, spying May Forrester standing before the mercantile. She held her head high, smiling smugly. "She said Grant would never marry me."

"That's utter nonsense."

I had stopped walking to face her. "Is it true? Are they…are they lovers?"

Maggie pursed her lips. "Well, that is the rumor, but you shouldn't listen to idle gossip."

"Did you know they were involved when you sent for me?" How could she do this? If she knew Grant's affections were already taken, why would she search for a mail order bride? It was entirely unfair.

"Her husband's on a cattle drive, and, when he returns, he's gonna take her over his knee."

"But you knew they were involved."

She sighed. "Oh, honey. I'm sorry. I was hoping he would let her go after he saw you. She's nothin' but trouble."

The ugly words May had uttered drifted through my mind. I wasn't naïve. I knew men sought comfort from soiled doves and widows, but I never expected to be confronted in such a manner and in a public place. It had cast a pall upon my day; all the pleasure I had experienced from the trip to town had vanished.

Mrs. Carson, sensing my distress, put her arm around my shoulder. "You should mention this to Grant. Tell him how badly you were treated by that woman. Shame him into changing his ways."

I had no intention of doing any such thing, and I did not want to discuss this unfortunate situation any longer. "Yes, we'll talk later."

"Good girl. You'll have it all sorted by supper."

But, I knew this would not happen, and, as the day progressed, I'd begun to feel downtrodden over the incident, wishing it had never occurred. Grant treated us to lunch at the only restaurant in town, the fare consisting of chicken salad with capers and applesauce cake. I struggled to contribute to the conversation, because it felt like I had died a small death. If I did marry him, I would have to compete for his affections. He was in no position to offer for me, because his heart was elsewhere.

The situation was even bleaker once we reached the ranch. Grant, sensing my unhappiness, followed me into the house. "What's the matter, Rebecca? You were in fine spirits this morning. You look like somebody shot your dog."

"It's...nothing." I did not want to tell him about the incident at the mercantile. "I've just...developed a headache. That's all." I sat on the sofa, willing the tears away, but knowing I would have to retire to my room soon.

He sat next to me holding his hat in his lap. "Was it somethin' I said?"

"It's the situation. It's rather impossible. We never spoke until a few days ago. All those letters were false. You didn't write them. I shouldn't expect anything from you. It's wrong. For all I know, you could be in love with someone else." I wondered how he would react to that.

He looked thoughtful. "I should tell you somethin'. You'll find out one way or the other anyhow. I've been…seein' a married woman. But I know there's no future there. I never should've gotten involved, but it's a little late now. Now you know my big secret."

"And you still want to marry me?" I could hardly believe this.

"I…do."

"What if we…if we have nothing in common? We've had a walk yesterday, but we hardly talked about anything, other than agreeing on a wedding date. What if you don't like me after it's all said and done?"

He grinned. "What's not to like? You're a handsome woman, and you're kind and pleasant to be around. I'm sure we'll find some common ground…at some point."

"I suppose."

"But?"

"Shouldn't we…feel some sort of affection? I

know this might be asking too much, but…we've never held hands or danced or any of those other things." Whenever I was in any proximity to Charlie, he always managed to touch me. Grant seemed to take great pains to lean away from me; his knees were to the other side.

"Now you got me confused. You came here expectin' to marry the same day we met."

"I know, but I thought I knew you. I thought it was you I had been writing to all these months. In the letters, you said how ardently you were looking forward to kissing and holding me."

"Is that so." His grin was charming, as he leaned in a fraction. "Sounds like ma was pretty darn frisky in those letters. I'd like to read them one of these days."

I blushed furiously. "Well, I'm…oh, never mind. Forget I said anything."

"No, you're right. I should make some sort of an effort to…romance you."

"I would never force that on anyone."

"But, it's an important part of the courtin' process." His look was considering. "I should kiss you."

He drew near, his lips meeting mine, while he opened his mouth slightly. Never having been kissed before, I was suddenly fraught with confusion, not knowing where I should place my hands or if I should open my mouth. The kiss ended a moment later, as he drew away and we stared into each other's eyes. It was a clumsy and uncomfortable experience, which left me wondering if, perhaps, he did not find me appealing. I would not voice these questions out loud. I glanced at the doorway. Charlie stood there glaring at us.

"Sorry to interrupt this tender moment."

"Not at all." Grant got to his feet. "What can I do for you?"

"I've been told to fetch water and somebody's gotta get the ham outta the smokehouse."

He grinned. "Ah, farm duties never end. I'm just the man you're lookin' for."

"Well, if you can tear yourself away from Miss Hart, your help would be mighty appreciated." His look was pointed. "Can you part with your fiancé, Rebecca?"

I stood as well, smoothing my skirts. "Of course." Memories of that underwhelming kiss flitted across my mind. "I'm sorry I kept you."

"We can talk about this later," said Grant.

"Yes, I'd like that." But those words sounded hollow to me.

They left the room a moment later, while Shindy ambled in, jumping onto the sofa. I sat next to him, petting soft fur. "What a mess. What am I going to do? If this doesn't work, I can't go back east. I can't live with my sister." He licked my hand, resting his head over my thigh. "Well, you're not helpful at all."

After dinner, we sat before the fire talking, while I held a book, but I wasn't paying attention to the words. Mrs. Carson toiled away at her knitting, while Grant and Charlie laughed about old times. Shindy was at my feet, laying over both of them, while he slept. I had hoped to speak to Grant again alone, but it was not meant to be. He seemed preoccupied, checking a silver watch he withdrew from a pocket often, and by nine, he got to his feet.

"Sorry, folks, but…the boys and I got a game tonight."

Maggie gave him a look. "You don't gamble."

"Well, I promised Adam I'd put in an appearance. The pot's fifty dollars, and I'm determined to win."

"I wish you didn't have to go," she said. "You've hardly spent any time at home at all lately."

He had already moved towards the door, snatching his hat off a brass coat stand. "I know. I'll be back…later." He glanced at me. "I sure did enjoy talking to you earlier, Rebecca."

"It was nice."

"I'll be seein' y'all."

Charlie scratched his chin. "Have a safe trip to town."

"Thanks, I will."

I suspected he was going to be with his lover, although I did not want to think of it that way. After another half an hour, I excused myself, leaving the house for the privy out back, while the moon shone overhead in a bright ball of iridescent light. When I returned to my room, I found Shindy on the bed.

"Oh, you annoying dog," I griped, while unbuttoning my dress. Once I had changed into my nightclothes, I pushed on his rear-end to get him to move. "Come on now. Off you go." He looked at me with those glossy black eyes, yawning. "You can't sleep here." Giving up for the moment, I undid my hair by pulling out the pins. After I had brushed through the tangles, I again tried to dislodge the dog. "Up and at 'em. Let's go." He sniffed my hand, licking me. "For heaven's sake." I got into bed, intending on reading for a while. "Fine, you pesky thing, but when I'm finished with this book, you have to go." Shindy repositioned himself, resting his head on my lap. A short while later, a rap on the door pulled me out of the story. "Yes?"

The door swung open, revealing Charlie. "I thought so." He looked peeved, yet there was humor in his eyes. "You stole my dog again."

"No, I haven't. He won't leave. You're more than welcome to him."

"You two look mighty comfy."

I closed the book, staring at the man before me, noting the flannel shirt, with the sleeves rolled up to the elbows. His hair was tousled, looking windblown. "Shindy lacks manners."

"It's a family trait."

"You shouldn't be in my room, sir." Yet, it was thrilling having him here.

"Why not? I've come to get my stolen dog."

I had been petting Shindy, as his soft, furry ear was in my hand. "He's wearing me down, Charlie. He's charming."

"That's not a half bad idea."

"You should've trained him better."

"One of my many failings." His smile was mischievous. "He's a lucky dog; he really is. I'd want to be in this bed too."

Eleven

I had startled her with that announcement, but it had been the truth. There she was, petting Shindy with those pretty fingers of hers, while all I could think about was having them in my hair, while I kissed her. After having seen the exchange with my brother earlier, it was all I could think about.

"You're being impertinent, Mr. Carson."

"I know. I'm sorry."

"I think I'm done with this book."

"What is it?"

"A collection of poems."

"Ma says you finished the accounting."

"I did. You've a surplus of four hundred dollars."

"That can't be. We're in the red by a thousand."

"No."

"I'll have a look at it tomorrow."

"Be my guest, but I checked the math three times. You really need someone who can manage those ledgers better."

She was smarter than she let on, but I had already begun to suspect it. "All right."

"Will you thank me?"

"I suppose I should. Thank you."

"You're welcome."

She hadn't kicked me out of the room yet, or the dog. "You went to town today. I spoke with ma about it. She said you were accosted by Mrs. Forrester." Her smile faltered.

"I don't wish to talk about it."

"What did she say to you?"

"Nothing."

"I can't imagine that."

"You knew about this, didn't you? You knew he was…carrying on with her."

"Everyone knows it. When her husband returns, he'll probably shoot him. I expect Grant to hightail it on outta here then."

"Even if he's married to me?"

"You'll be a widow before you know it."

"That's no laughing matter, Charlie."

She was clearly upset, as her eyes had taken on a watery sheen. "I'm sorry, but you really aught to know what he's been up to before you marry him."

"He still wants to go through with the ceremony."

"Uh-huh."

"I…" she glanced away, "don't know anymore."

"About marrying Grant?" Why did that please me so much?

"I'm not sure we have anything in common."

"Most married people don't. They learn to tolerate one another." I remembered my parents and their arguments, although it had always been over something unimportant. I laughed at the memory. Rebecca's sadness had transformed into anger, as she glared at me. "Now, don't look like that, sweetheart. I'm sure he'll behave himself, once he's married."

"I suppose."

"What else is the matter? You look like you're about to cry."

"I have serious doubts about…everything."

Now this was interesting. "Like what? You can tell me anything." I sat on the edge of the bed, leaning in a fraction. At this proximity, I could smell her perfume.

"I don't know if I can trust you either. You seem to take pleasure in my discomfiture. You're laughing at me now."

"All right. I'll try to stop doin' that."

"What's so funny, sir?"

"Nothin'."

"Something is."

I sighed. "I just think you're a little crazy for comin' all this way to marry someone you've never met before. I can't see that being a good way to start a marriage."

"But you just said most couples don't know anything about each other."

"Never mind what I said. What do I know?" She stared at me with those luminous, dark eyes. I would have killed to know what she was thinking. "You kissed him. At least you did that. You can't get a kiss through a letter."

"That's true."

"I'm sorry I interrupted your...tender moment."

"It was...not all that tender."

Now *this* had my attention. "What was that?"

"Oh, nothing." She stared at Shindy's ear, as she rubbed it. The dog had been basking in her ministrations; his eyes had rolled into his head, while his tongue hung out.

"I've heard it through the grapevine that Grant's quite the kisser."

She shrugged. "I haven't much experience in that. I wouldn't know."

"He used to chase all the girls around the schoolyard. None of 'em offered any objections."

"I see."

"You tellin' me you weren't swept off your feet?"

"I think people make a bigger deal of those sorts of things then they should. After all, it's just two mouths meeting."

"Um…there's a lot more to a kiss than that."

"I…suppose."

"It don't sound like you enjoyed it all that much. Maybe if you had somethin' to compare it to, you'd think differently."

"It's too late now. I'll be married on Saturday, and I don't intend on kissing strange men."

"How about just this man?" I pointed to myself. "How about I show you what a real kiss is." To my vexation, she began to laugh.

"Oh, that's rich! You'd just love that, wouldn't you? You'd give your eyeteeth to take advantage of me."

She was perceptive, which should not have come as a surprise. I had been angry after walking in on them in the parlor earlier, hating that my brother had kissed her. I would have given anything to be in his place. The air crackled with a vibrant, potent energy. Was I the only one who felt it?

"You're quite the charmer, aren't you?" A teasing glint shone in her eyes.

"I'd like to charm you…right outta that nightgown."

"Oh, Charlie!"

I had uttered exactly what I had been thinking. Before she could rail at me for voicing my thoughts, I grasped her face, intent on tasting those full, inviting lips. She gasped, clearly stunned, while I claimed her, giving into the desire that had been burning within me since the first moment we met. Her arms snaked around my neck and those thin, pale fingers drove through the strands of my hair. She uttered something that sounded like a denial, but it died in her throat. Nothing mattered now, as there would be no turning back. I explored her mouth, while she clung to me, kissing me with a fervor I found exhilarating.

She pushed me away. "Oh, you...shouldn't have." Her face had flushed to a dusty shade of pink.

Shindy took that moment to place his paw in her lap, as if reminding her that she was to continue to stroke him. He was wedged between us, his breath slightly foul.

"Just one more, Rebecca, please..." Not being able to help myself, I grasped her face, pressing my mouth to hers. She moaned softly, while I nibbled her neck, sucking and biting gently. The lobe of her ear was between my lips. She clutched at my shoulders, the tips of her fingers digging into the taut bands of muscle there.

"Really...you...must...stop..." She sounded

breathless.

"I think I've made my point." I gazed into her eyes, recognizing the look of surrender, but instead of feeling a sense of victory, I was angry that she still thought it pertinent to marry my brother. "What did you think of that?"

"It…was inappropriate." The dog took that moment to whine, his nose nudging her arm. "You're both rather demanding." His ear was in her hand again, while he laid his head in her lap contentedly.

I felt the most ridiculous urge to toss Shindy off the bed and take her into my arms, despite her protestations. I knew when a woman fancied me, and Rebecca had responded with enthusiasm and passion. That kiss would fuel my fantasies for nights to come. "I'm sorry you weren't impressed with my kissin' skills. I thought I did better than that." I needed her to admit that she wanted me. My ego demanded it.

"I don't think we should discuss this."

"It's been a while since I've romanced a lady. Maybe I've lost my touch."

Her attention was on Shindy; the dog was in heaven, his tongue hanging out of the corner of his mouth, while she scratched the top of his head. "I think it's time you took your dog and went to your room."

"That's a darn shame." I glanced at Shindy.

"Well, buddy, we've failed here. She didn't seem to like us all that much."

"I…wouldn't say that…"

That was all the encouragement I needed. "Up you go, you rascal." I shoved the dog from behind, bringing him to his feet. Although he was displeased with this, he jumped to the floor. "That's better." Without him in the way, I grasped Rebecca, kissing her fervently, while my arms went around her. She offered little resistance, as she moaned against my mouth. In a move as smooth as a dance hall Lothario, I had her on my lap…just where I wanted her. Without Shindy between us, I took full advantage, pulling her in even closer, letting her feel the extent of my desire.

"Oh, no, Charlie!" She gasped near my ear, while I ran my hands down her back, cupping the globes of her buttocks. "Stop that!" She pushed against me, scrambling from my lap. She was even more flushed now, and angry. "Y-you have to leave at once." She flung open the door, standing by it, while Shindy sauntered into the hallway. "Please go."

I got to my feet, resisting the urge to adjust my pants. "Things were only just beginnin' to get interesting."

"You've crossed the line." She lifted her chin a notch.

"You didn't seem to mind."

"Out! I'm going to pretend this didn't happen. You're not someone I can trust at all."

Now *that* angered me, as I knew it was a lie. "You got it all wrong, sweetheart. Of all the people around here, I'm the *only* one you can trust. I would never lie to you." She looked torn, her eyes filling with tears. I hadn't meant to upset her, but I had to defend myself against that accusation. "If you persist in marryin' Grant, fine. I won't stop you. If that's what you want outta life, it's yours to take. But just know this." I reached out to touch her, holding her face in my hands. "I think you're makin' a huge mistake. You're about to marry the wrong brother, darlin'."

I turned on my heel and left the room. I was certain that kiss had affected her, just as much as it had affected me. If she married Grant, I did not know how I could go on at the Carson Ranch, but one thing had become clear. My ungrateful wretch of a brother was about to marry the only woman I had ever loved.

Twelve

I stared at the door for a long time, while Charlie's words drifted through my mind. I could still feel the pressure of his lips and those soft, urgent kisses that I could not get enough of. The scent of sandalwood and musk lingered on my face and neck, while my traitorous body vibrated with an energy I could only classify as carnal. I had never been in such a state. I had never felt as out of control. It had taken every bit of willpower to push him from me and send him from the room, although I longed to snatch him right back.

Oh...goodness...

More confused than ever, I turned down the lamp and slid beneath the sheets, determined to sleep, although it was hard to come by. I tossed and fidgeted, not being able to find a comfortable position to lie in. Charlie's words lingered in my consciousness. *"You're about to marry the wrong brother, darlin'."*

The kiss I had shared with Grant had been chaste and reserved. None of these wild and conflicting emotions had surfaced. With Charlie, it felt as if I were drowning in pleasure. The feeling was warm, encompassing, and wondrous. Frustrated with myself, I punched the pillow angrily, wanting to put the entire episode out of my mind, but I knew it was hopeless. I would be married the day after tomorrow to Grant, and all I could think about was kissing Charlie.

I turned onto my back, staring at the ceiling. "What a muddle," I whispered. It would be another hour before I closed my eyes and drifted to sleep.

In the morning, I found Maggie in the kitchen. She held a bowl in her arms, using a wooden spoon to stir the contents. "Speak up now. Vanilla or chocolate cake, my dear?"

I glanced at her tiredly. "What?"

"Your weddin' cake. What flavor do you like?"

"Vanilla is fine. Do you need help with that?"

"This is the first batch. I plan to make two layers. Do you want more?"

"No, two is plenty. You could make the second layer chocolate."

Her eyes lit up. "Now there's an idea. That would satisfy everyone, wouldn't it?"

I sat at the table, reaching for a teapot. "Yes, it would."

"You look tuckered out, honey. Did you sleep badly?"

"I suppose I did."

"I'm sorry. Was the bed too lumpy? It's coming up on five years, and it probably needs re-stuffing."

"No, the bed…was fine."

"Would you like milk and sugar with that?"

"Yes, please."

She bustled around the kitchen, retrieving the items in question. "I've spoken to Pastor John, and he's reserved the church for us. I'm not certain how many people will attend, but they'll come for the cake." She smiled, the edges of her eyes creasing. "Nothin' like cake to reel 'em in."

Strangers would have a front row seat to the most important event of my life. "I knew it would be a small affair. I don't mind." I had come to Kansas to find a husband and secure my future. That goal was in sight, but why could I not feel any joy in it? What was the matter with me?

"Does your dress need pressing?"

"Yes. I'll do it as soon as I have breakfast." There was a loaf of bread on the table with a thick wedge of butter. I helped myself to a slice.

Charlie breezed into the room wearing denim pants and a striped tow shirt with the sleeves rolled up to the elbows. His expression was far too jovial, as he stared at me, smiling. "Good mornin', Rebecca. Did you sleep well?"

"Not especially."

"I slept like a baby."

"I'm…profoundly happy for you." I hated that knowing, intimate look in his eye. Taking a bite of bread, I lowered my gaze, staring at the tablecloth.

"Is Grant here yet?" asked Maggie.

"No, he isn't," said Charlie. "I'm headin' to town later. I'll try to find him."

"He's been dreadfully irresponsible. I don't know what's gotten into him. He used to be a lot more dependable. I've got a list of things that need fixin'."

"I hear you." Charlie poured himself a cup of coffee, taking a seat next to me. "Well, one more day," he murmured. "You'll be a married woman."

I did not want to have this conversation. "Yes."

"You got everything you need for the weddin'?"

"I believe I do…except for a groom."

"Grant will be at the church tomorrow at eleven, with bells on," said Mrs. Carson. "Don't you worry about that."

"There are a few things I wanted to discuss with him beforehand. We've hardly had any time together."

"My brother is a man of mystery," quipped Charlie.

I gave him a sour look, which he noted with glee.

"Yes, ma'am. That man just keeps you guessin', don't he?"

"I can't see why, Mr. Carson." I itched to slap him, if only to remove that smug and irritating smile from his face. I hated that my insides tingled whenever he looked at me. I could still smell his fragrance around my neck, as I had neglected to wash there this morning.

"You look tired." The teasing smile had fallen. "You have a bad night?"

"I did."

"Wedding nerves?"

"Something like that."

"Second thoughts?" An eyebrow arched. "You can cancel the whole affair, if you want. You don't have to go through with it."

I sat straighter. "I came to Kansas to get married, sir. I was supposed to be married the first day."

"Yeah, but you know it was all a lie. Grant's a stranger to you. I think it would be wise to wait until you knew him better."

I was loath to admit it, but his reasoning was sound. However, the look in his eye openly challenged me to agree with him, which stoked my anger even further. I had always possessed a bit of a stubborn streak, and I was on the edge of unleashing it now. "Like you said, most married couples don't know each other well anyhow. Ignorance is bliss, isn't it?"

"Nope. Ignorance is just stupid. If I were gonna marry someone, I'd make darn sure we were compatible. My wife is gonna be my partner not only in my bed, but in my life."

It was difficult to be angry with him when he spoke like that. "What sorts of things are you looking for?"

"How often she expects me to go to church, for one. I've no problem with God, but I like to sleep in on Sundays occasionally."

"Would twice a month be acceptable?"

He grinned. "It would."

"The other question would be children, wouldn't it?"

"Yes."

"How many do you want?"

"I'd take 'em one at a time. Childbirth ain't a walk in the park. Too many women die. If God blessed me with one or two, I'd be happy. More is like icing on cake."

"What about respect?"

"What about it?"

"I couldn't live with someone, if they didn't respect me."

"Respect is earned."

"Yes, but there are basic kindnesses that shouldn't be overlooked, such as treating someone politely. I'll not tolerate being spoken to like I'm a child. I won't be lied to or neglected or cheated on. Those are things women shouldn't have to live with. I'd hate to find out later that he likes to hit me when he's drunk." Charlie stared steadily, digesting my words with sober acceptance.

"Oh, sweetheart," said Mrs. Carson. "Grant would never do that. You really should talk to him about these concerns. I raised my boys better than that." Charlie snorted. She placed the bowl on the table, glaring at him. "What was that, Mister?"

"All the love and care you poured into Wyatt and Bronson seemed to go right through them. They've got a long way to go before they'd come anywhere near to Rebecca's standards." He sat up straighter. "She'd be hard-pressed to find that in Grant as well."

He had voiced exactly what I had suspected, and I hated having my fears confirmed. In an attempt to lighten the mood, I said, "Well, they say reformed rakes make the best husbands."

"You read that in some insipid novel?" asked Charlie, laughing. "Bad boys are bad boys, and this family has more than its fair share of 'em."

"But look at you." Maggie's hands were on her hips. "You're a wonderful man, Charlie. You've always been a good boy. The youngest children are usually the wildest, cause the parents are just plain worn out by the time they're born. They let them get away with everything. But, you're not like that at all. You stayed to run the ranch, and I know you give Wyatt and Bronson money whenever they come around. It's why our finances are a mess afterwards."

"Just put that halo on my head right now." He grinned.

"I've plans to find you a wife too. You'd make some woman very happy."

"Er, don't do that." His expression hardened. "I like to know who I'm gonna marry, thank you."

This had my attention. "And what qualities are you looking for, if you don't mind me asking. I told you mine."

"Same as yours."

"That's not good enough. What exactly do *you* want in a wife?" I was not sure why this was so important, but I had to know.

He looked thoughtful, scratching the shorn beard on his chin. "I want a kind woman. I don't want to wake up to screeching and hollerin'. I like peace and quiet."

"And?"

"A clean house, good meals, and happy children."

"Anything else?"

"She's gotta want me."

"H-how do you mean?"

"She's gotta want me as much as I want her. I'd only marry someone I needed to kiss…often."

Heat rose to my cheeks. "I…see."

He leaned nearer, murmuring, "I'd expect faithfulness too, but also forgiveness."

"My goodness, Charlie," said Maggie. "For bein' the youngest, you sure are the most mature of all your brothers. They could learn a thing or two from you. Maybe I should've gotten the wife for you first. I had no idea you were so ready."

His eyes were on me. "I didn't know either…"

Thirteen

By the time I had washed and changed into fresh clothes, it was almost time for supper. There had been no sign of Grant, and I was about to explode with fury. He had no business marrying Rebecca tomorrow, none at all!

After leading Sonny from the pasture, I placed the bridle over her head, getting ready to ride to town. It was a warm night, while the stars had only just begun to emerge, sunset having cast orange and purple shadows across the clouds. It was the kind of evening perfect for sitting on the porch with a glass of whiskey, rocking back and forth. That luxury would not be mine tonight, because I had an unruly and unpredictable brother to hunt down.

"Where are you going?" asked ma, who had come up behind me.

"Gotta find Grant."

"I'm worried."

I glanced over my shoulder. "You should be."

"Everything's all set. The cake's done, the dress is pressed, but I don't know about that brother of yours."

"I'm gonna have a word with him."

"He's with that woman, isn't he?"

"Yep."

"I thought bringing Rebecca into the fold would help him see the error of his ways, but I don't think it's made a darn bit of difference. He's determined to carry on with her. That husband of hers is gonna shoot him cold."

"Shoot him dead, you mean."

She touched my sleeve. "Please remind him of the importance of family. We splintered horribly after your pa's death, and then the war put another spoke in the wheel. Things have never been the same. Someone has to run the ranch, and it shouldn't all be on you."

I tossed a blanket over Sonny. "I'll see what I can do."

"If he fails to appear tomorrow—"

"Don't think like that." I placed the saddle on the blanket, working to fasten the front cinch. "I'm gonna do what I can. You can't force a man into marriage, Ma. It's a recipe for disaster."

"You seem quite fond of Rebecca. Those

questions you were asking each other at breakfast. It's almost as if you were the ones gettin' married."

I had thought the same thing, but Rebecca was determined to follow through with marrying Grant. "Well, I don't know what to say about that. She's my brother's fiancé, like it or not." Ma had that calculating look in her eye. "Don't go there," I warned. "Quit tryin' to play matchmaker. You've no skill in this area whatsoever."

She smiled slightly. "Don't be so sure about that. I think my plan might work beautifully, just not exactly like I thought."

I tied off the latigo with a Texas T knot. "Well, that's all fine and dandy, but I got this chore to get to. I hope I can find him," I muttered.

"He better not have left town."

"To shirk his responsibilities?" This was laced with sarcasm. That was one move all my brothers had perfected. They were good at stirring up trouble and then running away. I stepped into the stirrup. "I'm off."

"Have a safe ride, Charlie, and hurry back."

I tipped my hat at her. "Yes, ma'am."

Sonny and I took off into a gallop a short while later, cutting across a field. The lights of Elm Hill blazed in the distance; the town was quiet, save for the saloon, which hosted a dozen or more men every night, along with the occasional saloon girl. As I approached, I spied Grant's horse out front, and I dismounted, tying Sonny to the hitching post.

Entering the boisterous establishment, I was met with, "Hey, Charlie! Haven't seen you for ages." Trevor Port sat at the bar with his drinking buddy, Carl Hobbs. He lifted a glass. "Have a whiskey with us."

"Yeah, but I gotta see my brother first." I glanced around, spying him at a table in the back. "I'll talk to ya boys later."

"You celebratin' Grant's impending nuptials?" asked a gray-bearded man.

It seemed everybody in town knew what was happening. "If all goes well." This was met with laughter. "Save a barstool for me."

"Sure will," said Carl.

My boots clicked on the wooden floor, as I strolled across the room, passing several gaming tables and two sporting women, who smiled flirtatiously.

"How about a dance, sir?" asked the younger of the two.

"Maybe later." Grant sat hunched over, his hat hiding his face. "Fancy finding you here." Lifting his head, I caught sight of a blue and black eye. "Whoa! What happened to you?"

"May's old man came home."

"He beat the tar outta you?"

"Sorta."

I took a seat, while a saloon girl approached. "Can I get you a drink, mister?"

"Two whiskeys, please."

She smiled, revealing a missing tooth. "Anything else?"

"No, honey, but maybe later." I had no intension of hiring the services of any of the women here tonight. After she had sashayed to the bar, I asked, "What the hell is going on?"

"I got my butt handed to me. What do you think's goin' on?"

"You're supposed to be gettin' married tomorrow morning."

"I remember. I might be drunk, but I'm not…stupid."

Two glasses came our way. "Thanks, honey."

"I can sit on your lap for a dollar," she asked suggestively, playing with the purple balboa around her neck.

I smiled politely. "Not at this minute. I need to have a word with my brother."

"All right. Just give me a holler anytime you want somethin' else." She walked away, winking over her shoulder.

Removing my hat, I hung it over the back of the chair, while running my fingers through my hair. "What in the blazes is goin' on?"

"Just what it looks like. I'm havin' a drink…or two."

"So, Mr. Forrester returned tonight and caught you with his wife."

"Not exactly."

"How'd you get that shiner then?" He sat back in the chair, slouching. There were scratches up and down his arms. "You're all tore up."

"That's from scaling the side of a buildin'." He grinned, coughing.

"Why don't you start at the beginning?"

"I was tryin' to say my goodbyes to May. I really was. After she put her kids to bed, I came in the back door." He took a sip of whiskey.

I smirked. His words brought up scandalous connotations. "And?"

"I told her in no uncertain terms that it was over. My ma's arranged a marriage for me, and, come Saturday mornin', I was gonna be a changed man."

"Go on."

He sighed. "Then she started to cry."

"You didn't fall for crocodile tears, did you?"

He'd pressed his lips together, a guilty look on his face. "Er…I'm not sure."

"Then you left her?"

"The thought of sayin' goodbye…" his eyes took on a faraway quality…"I just couldn't do it. She cried like a baby, swearing that she loved me and needed me. How was I supposed to resist that? The next thing I knew, we were in her bed…er…without our clothes on."

I rubbed my forehead, feeling twinges of a headache emerging. "Then?"

"Then the front door slammed, and her husband shouted, "Whose horse is that? I never bolted so fast outta a bed before, trying to get my pants on. I was hoppin' around on one foot, while May dressed."

The picture he painted brought out a smile on my face, but I shouldn't encourage this dastardly behavior. "And?"

"I crawled through the window! A two-story window! I tossed my hat, belt, and boots out and stood on a ledge that was no more than four inches wide, if that. You know I never liked climbing trees like Bronson and Wyatt. I ain't no trapeze artist."

"Looks like you made it down fine."

"I got all tore up trying to hold onto the siding. I've got splinters everywhere. Molly Pale lives next door. I got into one of her windows, but she caught me."

Now I laughed in earnest. Molly Pale was a hefty woman—a widow, who was well known for her no nonsense personality. "Oh, lordy."

"She came at me with a broom! There I was holdin' my pants up, cause my belt was in the backyard. I didn't have shoes on or my hat. I tried my best to go around her, reassuring her that I had mistakenly entered the wrong house, but she wouldn't have any of it."

I threw back my head laughing.

"Then she starts screamin' like the banshee, sticking the broom in my face, but now she was usin' the other end. That's when I got the black eye. I managed to get by her and race down the stairs, but I was sore tired after that."

"And you came here to recover?" My belly ached from laughing.

"Certainly." He lifted the glass. "Here's to close calls, pretty women, and…the women we can't live without."

"You're gonna show up at the church lookin' like something a horse ran over. What do you think Rebecca's gonna think about that?"

"It can't be helped."

"You're gonna be at the wedding, right?"

"Absolutely." He downed the contents of the glass.

"You gonna be sober?"

"Maybe by mornin'."

I had my doubts. "May's husband is home now. It's time she starts to behave herself and take care of her man and her children."

"She knows that."

"You've both been awfully irresponsible."

"I can't believe I'm being lectured by my little brother."

"Somebody has to talk some sense into you."

"You got nothin' to worry about. I'll be at the church tomorrow with bells on. I'm a reformed man. I'm ready to commit myself…to…Rachel."

"Rebecca."

"Right, Rebecca." He hiccupped.

I waved to the saloon girl, who sashayed over, a cloud of rose perfume lingering around her. "Yes, sir?"

"I think we need a bottle of whiskey."

"I'll get that straight away, sir."

Grant pounded the table, rattling the glasses. "Darn straight! That's what I'm sayin'! We *should* celebrate. Tonight's my last night of freedom. Might as well let our cups run over, eh?"

I nodded, eyeing him. "Yep. We'll take it one drink at a time, big brother. One drink at a time."

Fourteen

I had struggled to sleep through the night. A confusing jumble of thoughts had drifted through my mind until the early hours of the morning. Today was my wedding day. It was supposed to be the happiest day of my life, but a strange sense of melancholy had settled upon me, and it was profoundly worrying.

A rap on the door had my attention. "Yoho! Wake up," said Mrs. Carson cheerfully. "Rise and shine. I've a lovely scrap of lace for your veil."

"All right." I swung my legs over the side of the bed. "I'll be out in a moment." Spying myself in the mirror, a woman with bleary eyes stared back at me.

"There's coffee and tea. It's all waiting in the kitchen."

"Thank you."

I set about washing my face and hands and cleaning my teeth. Then I took a brush to my russet strands, working out the tangles. While thus occupied, I thought of Charlie leaving last night to find Grant. I had not heard him return, and I knew he wasn't home. Had he located my fiancé? Would Grant be at the wedding? I wished I had been able to speak to him more about things, but that opportunity had evaporated.

Once dressed, I joined Mrs. Carson in the kitchen, helping myself to tea and bread, while she chatted happily.

"I'm so pleased everything's worked out."

"Did Grant come home last night?"

She glanced over her shoulder. "It's not likely."

"Maybe Charlie didn't find him."

"Oh, I'm sure those boys were half seas over, but they'll be at the church on time. Charlie will see to it."

"Does that mean drunk?"

"Yes, my dear. I'm sure they were…very drunk."

"I had wanted to speak to Grant, but it seems I won't get the chance."

"You'll have plenty of time to do that once you're married."

That did not fill me with confidence. "I suppose."

"You seem a little low. Is something wrong?"

Oh, where do I begin? I'm far from home, at the mercy of strangers, and I'm about to marry the wrong man! "I'm rather tired. I didn't sleep well."

"You poor thing. I had weddin' nerves too." She brought over a plate of coddled eggs. "Here you are. I'm going to tidy up here and then get dressed."

"Will Charlie take us to the church?"

"I…" she hesitated, "am not sure. We might have to meet them there."

"I see." I would not have the opportunity to speak to Charlie either. I was going to confess to him…to tell him that I…adored him. The more I thought about it, the more I realized I was in love—quite hopelessly in love, just with the wrong brother. "I know what I'll do then," I murmured.

"Pardon?"

"Nothing. Sorry."

She smiled wistfully. "It's your special day. Please let me know if there's anything I can do to help you get ready." She caressed my face, which was unexpected. "I'm so happy you'll be my first daughter-in-law. I do hope more will follow. I pray they'll all be as lovely as you are, Rebecca. You're a wonderful woman, and I'm proud to have you in my family."

Her sincere speech had left me in tears. I got to my feet, hugging her. "Thank you, Maggie. That's so kind. I can't think of a better mother-in-law."

"Thank you for comin' to Kansas, honey. I know you're gonna end up happy with…one of my boys. " She squeezed me. "And I'm gonna have the most darling grandchildren. I just can't wait for that."

"Oh, my," I giggled, pulling away to look at her. She was shorter than I was by several inches. "Well, I'll try my best, but I can't promise anything."

"I know you will." She turned for the door. "Now I'd best get myself together. Let me know if you need help with your hair."

"I will."

"I left the veil on the bed."

"Thank you."

I found myself in the kitchen alone, staring at the metal pots that hung from hooks in the wall. It smelled of coffee and eggs; the aroma was comforting, but my thoughts were anything but. Shindy ambled over, sniffing my foot before sitting on the floor next to me.

"Hello, boy." I petted his head. "Where's your owner? Have you seen him?" I wouldn't get an answer, but I had to wonder where Charlie was and why he had not come home last night. I needed to speak to him quite urgently. "Oh, what am I going to do?" A soft ear was between my fingers. "I really like Charlie, Shindy. I think…I like him an awful lot. If I had my druthers, he'd be the one I'd marry." It was strange saying these words out loud, but I had needed to share them, even if the only one who heard was the dog.

After breakfast, I readied myself, wearing a cream-colored skirt with a fitted bodice. I had worn several layers of petticoats and a pair of white gloves. My hair was twisted into a heavy knot at the back of my head, held in place by dozens of pins. The veil, which was a square scrap of lace, went over my face. Glancing in the mirror, I looked like a bride. Now, all I needed was a groom.

"Aren't you lovely?" gushed Mrs. Carson, who stood in the doorway. "It all came together rather nicely, if I don't say so myself."

"I imagine."

"We'd best get going. Cutter's offered to drive us."

"Very well." I took one last look at my handiwork, seeing a face hidden by lace. "I'm as ready as I'll ever be."

Mrs. Carson smiled. "Now, there's the spirit."

The wagon waited out front, while Cutter helped us alight. I sat in the middle, with Mrs. Carson on the end. The veil helped shield me from the brightness of the sun, on this beautiful, perfect Saturday morning.

Derrick had come out to bid us farewell, standing by the side of the barn. "Good luck," he called.

"Thank you," said Maggie.

Inhaling the aroma of fresh hay with hints of clover, I braced myself for what would come today. I was on the precipice of an enormous change in my life, and the decision before me was momentous. Marriage was forever, and a girl had to choose wisely. The ride to town wasn't long, and, as we trundled down the main thoroughfare towards the church, I gazed at the smattering of buildings and businesses. Most would remain open until early afternoon. The church was towards the end, the white steeple jutting out amongst a backdrop of prairie. There were several wagons and a carriage parked nearby. People had gathered to witness my nuptials, but they were all strangers to me.

Mrs. Carson grinned. "I invited some folks."

I wasn't sure if I should be gladdened by this announcement or horrified. "How…nice." The wagon came to a stop, while Cutter jumped from the seat. He helped us alight, holding my gloved arm. "Thank you."

"I'll see if my boys are here." Mrs. Carson took to the steps, disappearing into the building.

Not knowing what I should do, I remained before the church with Cutter to keep me company, although I knew nothing about the man other than he worked at the Carson Ranch. A woman approached, and I recognized her instantly. "Mrs. Aberdeen!"

"Don't you look lovely!" She hugged me. "Russell and I are just thrilled for you. I'm so happy we were able to share in your happy day."

Tears were in my eyes. "Thank you." Then I felt badly, knowing that she would witness the debacle, as I wasn't sure myself if I would become Mrs. Carson today. There were still too many unanswered questions, and I was running out of time. "Thank you for coming. It's so good to see a friendly face."

"Now, why the tears?"

"I'm…just…emotional."

Maggie had returned, but her expression was puzzling. "Um…my…oh, dear."

I glanced at her. "What?"

"Well," she wrung her hands, "I suppose we should get started."

"The groom's here?"

"Um…yes."

"I really would like a word with Grant, if I may. I have…something important to discuss with him."

"It's bad luck to see the groom before the wedding," said Mrs. Aberdeen. "I'm sure whatever you need to say can wait."

My stomach dropped. "It's dreadfully important."

"Come along, Rebecca." Mrs. Carson waved to me. "The Wedding March has begun."

Now I was on the verge of panic. "But—"

"Cutter's offered to walk you down the aisle. It's going to be fine." She smiled kindly. "You'll be right where you should be. Trust me."

This was worse than I thought, and I would not be able to talk to Grant—to tell him that I did not want to marry him. *Oh, my stars! What a disaster!* All eyes were on me, and my moment of reckoning had arrived. With great reluctance, I took to the stairs, feeling that each step brought me closer to doom. I could dash into the prairie and run away, but it wouldn't solve any of my problems. Breathing in a deep, steadying breath, I tried to calm myself, never believing that I would feel this petrified on my wedding day.

A piano played the Wedding March, while there were quite a few people in attendance, most of them strangers. The smell of incense lingered along with the scent of rose water perfume of the ladies present. The mixture produced a twinge of queasiness, as my belly turned over. Because of the veil, my vision was not as clear as it should be, although I could see my fiancé standing at the front of the church with Pastor John. His features were somewhat blurred, and, as I began to make my way towards him, things slowly, steadily came into view.

I gasped. The man waiting for me below the pulpit wasn't Grant Carson. My heart began to pound wildly, while the shock of what I was seeing raced through me, like a fire across an acre of grassland.

"Charlie?"

He grinned crookedly. "Yes, ma'am."

Fifteen

It was Charlie!

He cut a fine figure in a pair of tan trousers, a waistcoat with a matching frock coat, and a black necktie that stood out against a crisp white shirt. His hair had been combed back, while a grin revealed a mischievous smile.

"What in heavens?"

"I'm sorry, but I can't let you marry Grant, honey. It wouldn't be right."

The thrill of seeing him had yet to wear off. "It's not?"

"No, Rebecca. You know it isn't."

Pastor John glanced between us. "Is something amiss?"

"Not at all," assured Charlie. "The right people are gettin' married today."

I could not argue with that statement, knowing

that he was right. He felt the same way about me. There could be no other explanation as to why he had taken his brother's place, but I had to be sure. "You don't have to do this," I whispered.

"I don't. But there's no way I'm lettin' my good-for-nothin' brother marry the woman I love. That ain't gonna happen. You're mine."

He had spoken those words with confidence, his look as earnest as I had ever seen. Tears flooded my eyes, as I was overcome by emotion. I tilted precariously, needing something to hold on to. Strong hands grabbed me.

"There now, honey. Take it easy."

I was in his arms—exactly where I wanted to be. "I had hoped to talk to you this morning. There was so much I needed to say."

"You'll get your chance, Rebecca. We got a lifetime to talk things out."

"You—you really want to do this?"

He held my face, although it was concealed beneath the veil. "Yes, sweetheart. I really do."

The timber in his voice sent a shiver down my spine. "I…I'm glad. That's what I wanted to talk to you about. I…was so worried. I can't marry Grant."

"There's no way I'd let you. He's in no condition to offer marriage to anyone, least of all you. You were meant for me."

The pastor cleared his throat. "Well, then.

Perhaps we should commence with the ceremony. All parties seem agreeable. Are there any other objections?" He glanced at me. "Miss Hart?"

"No, sir."

"Mr. Carson? Shall we begin?"

He grinned. "Please do. The Lord's stamp of approval will seal the deal."

It was unseemly to cry like this, but I could not stop the tears as they slid down my face. What had begun as a horribly depressing morning had transcended into a dream come true. I would not have to speak to Grant after all and confess that I was in love with his brother.

As Pastor John spoke, I had eyes only for Charlie, who continued to grin, his expression never wavering. Once I had repeated my vows, he reached into his pocket and withdrew a simple gold band, which was then placed upon my finger. Stunned, I marveled at the fact that he had planned to do this all along.

"I now pronounce you man and wife."

Cheers rang out, as Charlie drew me into his arms; his mouth was near my ear. "I'm a lucky fella." He lifted the veil, revealing my tear-stained face. "I hope those are tears of joy." He wiped the wetness away with the pad of his thumb.

"They are." I had to know something. "What happened last night?"

"I plied Grant with whiskey. He's sleepin' it

off."

"I don't love him in the least, Charlie. I…" It was awkward that the preacher stood behind us listening. "I love you."

His grin was enormous. "I thought so."

"We're far better suited."

"Yes, we are. Any woman who could love my dog like that is all right in my book." His look was teasing.

"Charlie," I giggled.

"Congratulations," gushed Mrs. Aberdeen, as she hugged me. "I'm so delighted for you, my dear."

"Thank you."

Mrs. Carson took my hands, giving them a squeeze. "I'm not gonna complain that Grant's not standing here. I'm just thrilled one of my boys was lucky enough to marry you." She glanced at Charlie. "I knew you were better for her. I could see it from the start. There was always a spark."

"Yeah?" He nodded, glancing at me. "Can't disagree with that." Taking my gloved hand, he kissed it. "We should skedaddle to the reception. What do you say?"

"That's a marvelous idea."

He led me down the aisle, while people cheered. Someone threw rice outside, and felicitations abounded. The reception was held in the dining room of the local hotel, which had been decorated with white streamers and garland. We shared cake and wine, while Charlie was by my side, keeping a possessive hand on my lower back. I was startled when Grant suddenly appeared, looking the worse for wear, his clothing rumpled. There was a purple bruise beneath one eye.

"You done well," he said, shaking my hand. "I'm…" he glared at Charlie, "sorry I couldn't make it."

"You were in no condition to marry this woman."

"No, I wasn't. Not when you kept ordering whiskey. You did that on purpose."

"You bet I did."

"I…was gonna honor ma's promise. I was." He glanced at me. "I'm sorry I disappointed you."

"It's all right. You and I…I don't think we would've been a good fit."

"Maybe, once you're done runnin' around with May Forrester, you'll find a woman to settle with."

"Shush!" he muttered. "Don't say that so loud."

"What happened to your eye?" I asked.

He shuffled his feet, glancing downwards. "Um...bar fight."

Charlie patted his back. "You're free to sow those wild oats again."

"It's clear I've been given the mitten." Grant's smile revealed he wasn't too aggrieved. He took my hand. "You look beautiful. I'm glad you married Charlie. He'll do right by you." He glanced at his mother, who had overheard the conversation. "Don't do this again!" An accusing finger pointed in her direction.

Her eyes widened. "What on earth do you mean?"

"No more mail order brides, you hear? Don't go sendin' out those silly letters. I don't need help finding a wife. Is that clear?"

"Of course, Grant. I won't do it again. I promise." She winked at me.

Charlie whispered in my ear, "I want to be alone with you. How soon can we leave?"

The husky tenor in his voice sent a shiver down my spine. "I'm not certain."

"We've had cake and wine. I just want to go."

Maggie smiled. "Then leave. You needn't wait a minute longer."

"Thank the Lord."

I giggled, "What will we do now?"

"I'm takin' you home." He grasped my hand, pulling me towards the door. "Thanks for comin', folks! Enjoy the cake and wine. Rebecca and I are grateful you could share in our happy day."

Cheers rang out, as I was led from the building into the blinding sunlight. We hurried to Sonny, who had been tethered nearby. I sat sideways, while my husband held me, his arm firmly around my midsection. I glanced at him, smiling. His gaze drifted to my mouth, where he kissed me lightly.

"By mighty," he murmured. "I can't wait to be alone with you." We trotted through town, while interested glances followed us.

"Then we really should hurry."

"Hold on!" The horse bounded forward, as we cut across a field.

I laughed out loud, while the wind loosened my hair. Whatever misgivings I had felt earlier had vanished, leaving me with nothing but happiness and gratitude. Although Charlie and I had not known one another for very long, I knew in my heart that I had married the right brother.

We approached the house within moments, Derrick running out to greet us. I slid from Sonny, my feet touching the ground. "I'll take her. Congratulations, you two." He smiled kindly.

"Thank you," I said. Shindy ambled over, rubbing against my leg. "Hello, you."

"And a fine homecoming it is," said Charlie. I was in his arms then, as he had lifted me. "Your castle awaits, my lady."

"Oh, my word!"

"I apologize in advance, cause my room's a mess. Maybe…we should go to yours."

"It's fine. I don't mind either way."

"Yours it is." We headed for the door. I fumbled with the knob, while he shoved it open with his foot. He brought me down the hallway to my room, depositing me on my feet. "Here we are, Mrs. Carson."

I didn't know what to say, as a sudden bout of shyness gripped me. "What…will we do now?"

He tossed his hat to a chair. "Whatever you want." Sitting on the bed, he began to remove his boots. "For starters, why don't we make ourselves more comfortable?"

I was about to close the door, but Shindy arrived, jumping onto the bed. "Oh, no."

"I can't deal with him at the moment." Charlie gave the dog a shove. "Out with you, boy. You can come back later." Shindy was none too happy about this, as the door was closed in his face. He whined in the hallway.

"Poor thing."

"I'm not in the mood to share my woman right now." Charlie held out a hand. "Come here."

I went to him. "Yes?"

"You got way too many clothes on."

"I do?"

"Yep." He began to work the buttons on the bodice, impatiently undoing them one-by-one. "This could take all day."

"Sorry." I threaded my fingers through his hair. "I was so worried."

"About what?"

"About having to marry Grant."

"I can't believe you're not in love with my brother. Half the women in town are in love with him."

"That's troubling." I was half-teasing.

"But, honestly, he's not ready to marry anyone at the moment. He's stuck in, good as a tick, with that Forrester woman. Nothin' good will come of that, but it's not my lesson to learn."

"I know. I'd hate to be married to someone who was in love with someone else."

"It's a thorny situation. I didn't want you messed up in it." The bodice was loose now, although many layers of clothing were beneath. He worked on the blouse.

I glanced at my hand. "When did you get this ring?"

"This mornin'."

"You did?"

"Yes, ma'am. The mercantile had a few to choose from."

"It fits perfectly." The gold glowed warmly. "I love it."

"I'm glad."

"I'm so happy, Charlie."

He grasped me, as we fell to the bed. His face was in my neck. "I'm gonna have to thank ma for meddlin' in our lives. She didn't get a wife for Grant, but it sure worked for me."

"Yes, it did," I giggled.

"Now, I beg you, help me with this corset. It's gettin' on my nerves. I don't know why women have to wrap themselves up like this."

Sixteen

Getting Grant drunk had been a means to an end. Knowing that he did not love Rebecca, not nearly as much as I loved her, I could wipe my conscience clean for ruining his wedding. I had an inkling from the very first moment I met her, standing there at the train station, that she was destined to be mine. There had always been a connection, a thread of recognition, that traveled back and forth between us, alerting me to the fact that there was something about her I could not resist.

My wife's glorious skin was revealed after each article of clothing had been removed. It was like unwrapping a present, a very personal gift, meant only for me. No one else would ever gaze upon her in this way. My eyes skimmed over the curve of her hips and the flatness of her stomach with the tiny indentation of a bellybutton. A glorious swell of bosom had captured my undivided attention, but strands of hair had fallen upon them, hiding their intriguing beauty.

"What about you? Am I going to be the only one without clothes on?"

Wanting to put her at ease, I held out a blanket. "Take this."

"Thank you."

While unbuttoning my shirt, I glanced over my shoulder. She sat with the blanket to her chin, gazing at me. I had a question. "What if Grant had been standin' with the preacher instead of me?"

"I would've told them to cancel everything." Her expression was solemn. "I couldn't marry him, Charlie. He was entirely wrong for me."

"I can't agree more." My pants were on the floor, while I kept my shirt and drawers on, sliding beneath the blanket.

"It's not fair. I'm naked and you're not."

Her words were teasing, yet I caught vestiges of a seductress. "Is that so?" I turned towards her, feeling only skin, which sent a shot of heat through me. Far from shy, she pressed herself against my chest; her face was in my neck. I could feel every glorious inch of her.

"At least it's light out. I'm glad I can see you."

"You're not feeling self-conscious?"

"We can dispense with modesty now. We're

good and married. We won't have a sheet between us, will we?"

"I love your sense of humor, Rebecca. It's appealing, just like everything else about you."

"Maybe," she purred. "You're shy. You're the younger brother, after all." Her hand was on my chest, moving the shirt aside. "You've so much hair."

"Honey, men are hairy."

An eyebrow lifted. "Everywhere?"

"You'll just have to find out for yourself, I guess." She rubbed her cheek against my chest, which left me tensing with anticipation. My anatomy was more than aware of her proximity. She pulled on the shirt. "Here, let me help you with that." A scratch at the door was followed by a whine. "That annoying dog." I tossed the shirt to the floor. "There, is that better?"

"I don't know. Let me see." She leaned over me, her hair tickling my chest. "Look at those tiny nipples." One was squeezed between her fingers.

"Oh, Lord…" Her breasts were crushed against my ribcage. I wanted to grab her and kiss her senseless, but I did not want to rush, as she was exploring the unknown and enjoying it immensely.

"What about your drawers?" she asked.

"Honey."

"Yes?"

"You lost your shyness."

Her smile was teasing. "Is that a bad thing?"

"Not at all."

"Your mother expects grandchildren, Charlie. We're going to have to be naked to make them."

"Yes, darlin'," I chuckled.

All I wanted to do at that moment was kiss her. Those pink, soft-looking lips all but begged for it. She melted against me, wrapping her arms around my neck, while our tongues battled in silky wetness. My hands had a will of their own, as they felt her softness, skimming along her arms down towards her waist. Her buttocks were delightfully rounded and firm. She touched me as well, her hand sliding over my belly and lower.

"Rebecca?" I sounded hoarse.

"Yes?"

"I love you, darlin'."

"I love you too, Charlie."

I kissed her again, our breaths mingling. I held her face, while I nibbled on her neck, inhaling the fragrance of her sweet-smelling skin. She'd molded herself to me; a shapely leg was over my thigh, while she continued her explorations, touching me intimately.

"You're so beautiful," I murmured.

"Do you like this?"

"Yes, I do."

"You can touch me too."

"Is that so?"

"Can't you be serious for one moment?"

"I can." My hands did not need to be told what to do. I had already begun my own assessments, feeling the suppleness of her breasts, while pulling her even closer. "I can be very serious."

She had grown rather fearless, taking the initiative, while leaning over me, kissing my chest and suckling a nipple. Her silky hair was draped across me like a satin sheet. She seemed determined to not only kiss, but also taste, working her way towards my manhood. After she had satisfied that bit of curiosity, leaving me wound up tighter than a metal coil, we resumed our kisses, while I found her wetness, stroking her until she moaned.

"Oh, Charlie…"

That was all I needed to hear to settle between her thighs, joining with her in the most intimate way possible. She clung to me, her soft moans filling my ears, while I gave in to pleasure that far exceeded my expectations. Rebecca had shuddered in my arms, behaving in such a way to indicate that she had enjoyed the experience as much as I. It was satisfying to know that on her first attempt, she had not been inhibited in any way.

"Oh, my stars," she murmured.

"You seein' them?"

"Oh, stop it, you!" She pushed me. "You can't be serious for one moment."

I lay on top of her, still joined, but that wouldn't last for long. "I like poking fun, especially with you."

"That was nice, Charlie."

"You sore at all?"

"A little."

I fell to my side, reaching for her. "Well, ma wanted grandbabies."

"What if I'm making one at this minute?" She raised herself on an elbow, staring at me. "That'd be strange to think it might be happening right now."

"Not so strange."

"Nine months and…hum…"

"It doesn't always happen the first time."

Her smile was mischievous. "Then we'll have to do it quite often to make sure."

"I'd be more than happy to help with that."

"Well, I certainly can't do it without you." She beamed. "You're a rascal."

"I am, but the dog's worse."

"He hasn't stopped whining for a moment."

"Should I let him in?"

"Oh, goodness. Then there won't be any room in the bed."

"We might need a bigger bed."

"We haven't even discussed where we'll live."

"Here?"

"I suppose."

"You don't want to live at Carson Ranch?"

"I do, but we need a bigger bed and a nursery."

I grinned, feeling better than I could remember. I adored the way her hair fell around her shoulders. "Yes, ma'am."

She hugged me, murmuring, "I love you, Charlie. You make me so happy."

"You make me happy." And that was the God's honest truth. I'd never felt closer to anyone in my life, and the thought of being with Rebecca forever left me with a palpable sense of peace. "Remind me to thank my mother for meddling in our lives. I owe her…a huge favor."

She giggled in reply.

The End

Epilogue

Nine months later...

"There you are." I had come upon Mrs. Carson in the study, although she quickly hid whatever it was she was working on. "Charlie says to tell you the lumber arrived."

"That's good." She eyed me. "You're not goin' out and helping, are you? Not in your condition, I hope."

"No, I won't." I patted my bulging belly. "I made lemonade for the boys to drink. They'll be thirsty after they finish. It's so cold, though, maybe hot chocolate would've been better." She smiled furtively, which had me wondering what she was up to. "Are you working on the inventory?"

"No, my dear."

"I've updated the books. They should be fine."

"I know. Thank you."

She had roused my curiosity, as I took a few steps closer. "Is that a letter?"

"It is." Her hand was over the parchment. "And?"

"I didn't mean to pry."

"I write letters…occasionally." She smiled slightly. "I've found some success with letters."

"Like the ones you sent to me pretending to be Grant?"

"Maybe."

My eyes popped. "Oh! I knew it! What are you up to?"

"Nothing, my dear."

"You sneaky thing, Maggie. You're scheming again."

"No, I'm not."

"If you meddle again, your boys will never forgive you."

"Now that's not true at all. Look at you and Charlie. I've never seen a happier couple. In fact," she got to her feet, "you're always kissing. I thought that phase would've worn out by now, but it hasn't."

"I really like my husband. I can't help it."

"Well, see. I've made my point."

"What point?"

"My…er…letters served their purpose."

Now she had me worried. "Oh, you can't do that again. It's wrong to mislead a woman like that.

Please tell me you haven't spoken to another woman."

"I'm not doing anything." She smiled coyly. "Grant's doing it."

"No. Not again. You know he's not ready to settle down. He's involved with Mrs. Forrester. He must be in love with that woman."

"She's married! It's a scandal, Rebecca. I've got to do something to save him from himself."

"Oh, gosh, no. That's the worst idea yet. That poor woman will arrive here like I did and find—" But I had met Charlie, and I could never regret that. I was blissfully happy, and I would have a baby in the spring. All my dreams had come true and then some. "Oh, never mind."

"I know you're concerned, but I have faith that the right woman is waiting for Grant. All she needs is a train ticket. It worked so well for you and Charlie."

"I'll have to tell him about this."

"No, no. Not at all." She leaned in, whispering conspiratorially, "Let's keep this to ourselves."

"But you can't do that to a poor, unsuspecting woman. She'll come here with stars in her eyes, thinking she's about to marry her true love. Then she'll discover he's already in love with someone else."

"I know of the situation, Rebecca. I know it's a…challenge. I have faith my efforts will be rewarded. Again."

"It's just not right, and you know it."

"Well, if Grant won't see the light, maybe one of my other boys will interest her."

I had yet to meet Bronson or Wyatt. "They aren't here. No one knows where they are or what they're doing. Oh, what a mess. Please write a truthful letter. Tell her you've misled her. I beg you."

"It's a bit too late for that."

My heart sank. "What do you mean?"

"She's due to arrive in the spring."

"No. Please, no."

Her arm went around my back. "Now, don't you worry. It'll be just fine. Leave it all to me."

"You're a horrible woman." I was jesting, but I did feel awful for whomever it was she had tricked.

"I couldn't have asked for a better daughter-in-law and soon, I'll have that grandbaby I always wanted. Then Grant will be happily settled, and he'll walk the straight and narrow. I've so much work to do. My boys are the worst…er…the most wayward men I've ever met. Someone has to do something. They need strong women to take them in hand."

"But don't involve anyone else. Please. I'm sure there are some lovely ladies from Kansas who can help them."

"It'll be fine. Trust me."

Charlie appeared in the doorway. "Everything all right?" He'd removed his hat, which was in his hands.

"Your mother's up to her old tricks. I caught her writing a letter." Maggie gave me the evil eye. "She's trying to marry off Grant—again."

Charlie's mouth fell open. "NO, woman! Absolutely not!" I went to him, and he held me close. "Burn those letters. I'm not pickin' up another lovelorn woman from a train station."

"You're a fine one to talk. Look at you. You're perfectly happy, *and* you're about to be a father. You've no reason to complain. If anyone's meddling, it's that wife of yours. She has no business telling you or anyone else about my private affairs."

I knew she wasn't really angry. "You just don't know when to quit, do you?"

"Don't speak to me that way, young lady. I'm your elder. I know what I'm doing. One day, if you ever have boys like mine, you'll be quite desperate yourself to see them settled."

I glanced at Charlie. "It might be too late."

His look was pragmatic. "Should we warn Grant?"

"I...probably not. If he knew what was coming, he'd leave town."

Charlie's arm tightened around me, while his lips grazed my forehead. "You'll have to answer for this, Ma. It's your mess. Rebecca and I don't want any part of it."

"Not to worry," she said cheerfully. "It's all taken care of. Charlotte Mills is a lovely young woman who's in need of a husband. She's ready to take a chance on a new life in Kansas. Isn't that wonderful?"

Appalled, I could only stare at her.

Charlie was more vocal, uttering, "Tarnation!"

Preview of
A Mail Order Bride For Bronson

The Carson Brothers of Kansas
Book Two

Carson Ranch encompassed hundreds of acres in all directions, with two sturdy-looking farmhouses, matching barns, and other outbuildings. At first I had been gladdened by such good fortune, thinking that I might call this place home, but then I had remembered the circumstances surrounding my arrival, and the fact that I had not been corresponding with Grant Carson at all.

Swallowing the disappointment, I focused instead on the fact that Dudley and I were safe, far away from Virginia. The future would somehow work itself out, and this is what I would pray for each night. I had always been unlucky in life; it seems from the moment of birth. I hoped I had not found myself in another unpleasant situation, as nothing could be worse than what I had just fled from.

One of the first people I had met yesterday was Rebecca Carson, who was Charlie's wife. She had greeted me cheerfully with a surprisingly hearty hug, declaring, "Oh, you dear thing. Did Maggie tell you the circumstances of your arrival?"

"Yes. She confessed to writing the letters."

Charlie had rolled his eyes. "Please forgive us, Charlotte. My ma is...er...a character. She means well. Rebecca and I didn't know about it until recently, but then things were already in motion."

"I understand."

"Your son is adorable." Rebecca had gotten down on one knee to gaze at him. "What a bruise. My goodness. It looks just like your mother's."

It was awkward having to lie to people, but everyone had seen through it anyhow. Mrs. Carson knew my husband had been responsible. She guessed I had run away; she had to. She seemed like an astute person.

A golden colored dog ambled over, sniffing Dudley. "Oh, mamma! Look at that!" He'd grabbed the animal, squeezing him.

"Be careful. Some pets aren't all that friendly." Michael had a dog as well, but he was the most ill-mannered beast I had ever encountered. In a drunken rage, my husband had shot him. It was difficult to pity the animal, although it was yet another horrible night in my life. "He does seem friendly."

"Oh, he is," said Mrs. Carson. "You can hang all over him. He puts up with everything."

I had been given a tour of the house: the neat and orderly parlor, the kitchen with a large table in the center, and the bedroom, which I would share with Dudley, as I did not want to leave him on his own in a strange place. My home in Virginia wasn't nearly as nice; the roof always leaked, the wood so damp it smelled of mold, and our furniture had been broken more than once, leaving chairs slightly uneven and unsightly. The Carson Ranch was like a slice of heaven, clean and beautiful, set amidst verdant fields of corn and wheat. Dudley would love it here...if there were a possibility of us staying, and that was slim.

We had settled in that evening, unpacking and sharing a meal, which consisted of smoked ham, bacon, and potatoes. In the morning, I had helped Maggie with the laundry, and that chore had barely been completed before someone had arrived, garnering everyone's attention.

I had been in the parlor reading when I heard the voices. "Are we expecting someone?"

"I'm not sure," said Rebecca. "I'll go look."

I had followed minutes later, standing on the

porch, where I spied a rough-looking man talking to Charlie. Rebecca was on her way out to greet them. Something in his demeanor and the clothing triggered a memory. It wasn't until I started towards him, meeting his dark, brooding eyes, that recognition dawned. The shock came over me in waves, knowing that this was the scoundrel who had robbed us on the train. His shoulder had been injured, as his shirt was stained with dark, dried blood.

I blurted that he had robbed us, and he had not denied it. His face was darkened from several days' worth of stubble and dust from riding, leaving the blueness of his eyes to stand out, especially as they were surrounded by the thickest set of lashes I had ever seen on a man. I had not been able to get a good look at him on the train because of the bandana. Despite being dirty, there was something about him that I found inherently appealing.

It must be because he's a blackguard…no doubt…

"Let's go in and look at that arm," said Mrs. Carson. "It won't get any better out here." She'd held open the door, letting her injured son pass, while Dudley and I lingered.

"Are you all right?" asked Rebecca. "I don't know what happened on the train, but it must've been dreadful."

"It was."

Charlie seemed thoughtful. "I guess you won't want to attach yourself to a family such as ours. My older brothers are...er...bandits." He shrugged. "No beating around the bush on that one. It is what it is."

Knowing that I had arrived with several lies myself, I was in no position to judge. "I'm not going to the authorities, if that's what troubles you, sir. I...it was nothing. He stole my last ten dollars."

"And he'll return every penny with interest." Charlie held the door. "Please come inside." His look had soured. "I'm going to knock that mudsill in the head," he muttered.

"Well, your family is colorful," said Rebecca. "You've been warning me from day one about them."

"It's really enough now. The farm earns plenty for everyone. There's no reason to go around committing armed robbery and killin' people. No reason at all."

While Dudley played with Shindy in the parlor, I had gone to the room next to mine, watching as Mrs. Carson began to peel Bronson's shirt from his body.

"Ouch!" he groaned. "Take it easy."

"I'm gonna need that moonshine Wyatt left behind. It's the strongest liquor we have."

"I know where it is," said Charlie.

"Those stitches are uneven," said Rebecca.

"Whoever closed the wound did a dastardly job."

"I'm handy with a needle."

This announcement had garnered everyone's attention, especially Bronson, who glanced my way. "She's liable to get even by pokin' my eye out. I know I've done you wrong, darlin'. I'll give your money back. I swear."

It was the oddest thing, but despite the fact that he was a filthy, horribly mannered man, there was something about him that garnered my sympathy. "That would be gentlemanly of you, sir." Then I added, "I won't poke your eye out."

"Gosh, oh, my word." Mrs. Carson had uncovered the wound. Bronson was shirtless now, his chest lean, yet hardened with muscles and smattered with small scars. His belly was slightly concave, yet rippled with sinew beneath a thin layer of skin. "This is a bullet wound."

He grimaced. "It might be."

Laughter filled the room. "Oh, your reputation is well-deserved, sir." Amusement danced in Rebecca's eyes. "Here I thought I'd never meet the notorious Carson brothers, and, when I do, one's fresh off a robbery with a bullet wound. How fitting."

"Here's the moonshine." Charlie handed the bottle to his mother. "It's gonna sting like heck."

"Can you bring me a cloth and a bowl of water? I'll need scissors and needle and thread.

I've…oh, gracious. I've never sewn skin before. Maybe we need Doc Sewell."

"No! No doctors." Bronson struggled to sit. "No authorities. Just…just clean it up and cover it. That should do it."

"I'll put some hot water on," said Rebecca. "Does anyone want tea? I could use a cup myself."

"I'll sew it, if you want me too," I said. "I've stitched up worse." Expectant eyes stared at me. "I mean, I've some experience, is all."

Mrs. Carson got to her feet. "I'll find the items I'm lookin' for. Charlie won't know where they're at."

"Mamma!" Dudley raced into the room, grabbing my leg. "What's wrong with the bad man?"

"He's injured."

"He's a train robber, right?"

"Yes, I believe so."

These words seemed to bother Bronson, as his expression fell. He held out a hand. "Come here, squirt. I'm not *that* bad."

"You stole my ma's money."

"I did, but…" He had no excuse for his behavior, and he knew it. "I'll pay her back."

"You will?"

"Yeah."

"That's the right thing to do, mister."

"How old are you?"

"Five, sir."

"So I'm gettin' a lecture from a five-year-old?"

I stood over the bed, having crossed my arms over my chest. "It appears so."

Dudley drew near, eyeing the stranger's wound. "That looks disgusting. It's all red and oozing. It's still bleeding too."

"I know. It's what I get for being a bandit, I suppose."

"Will you stop now? Why you gotta go and rob trains anyhow? Isn't there something better you could do to earn money?"

The look of chagrin on Bronson's face was almost laughable. "I…guess I should consider another line of work. Are you sure you're only five-years-old, son?"

Dudley nodded. "You don't drink, do you?"

"I like a spot of whiskey every now and then, why?"

"Men are ugly when they drink. When I grow up, I ain't touchin' the stuff."

"Is that so?" He glanced at me. "I take it the boy's father is responsible for this?"

"That's really none of your business." I did not wish to discuss this particular topic. Mrs. Carson's appearance saved me from having to say anything else.

"What exactly is this woman doin' here?" He glared at his mother.

"She's Grant's fiancé."

"Is he aware of that?"

"Uh…in a way."

"I'd like a drink of that, if you don't mind."

"It's coffin varnish. I save it for wounds."

"Is there any whiskey?"

"I'm sure Charlie can get some."

Rebecca appeared in the doorway. "The tea's almost ready."

"Darlin', could you find some whiskey, please?" asked Bronson. "I'd greatly appreciate it."

She nodded. "For the pain. I'll go fetch it."

"Now, I'll open this up and wash it out. Then Charlotte can stitch it back up, if she wishes." She grinned. "Or she could just poke your eye out. It's not like you don't deserve it for robbing your brother's fiancé."

He stared at me. "I already apologized about that. Her kid's sure got an awful lot of opinions for someone so young."

"He's precocious and adorable, and I'd be very happy to have him for my second grandchild." She smiled brightly. "I know good people when I see them. She'll make one of my boys very happy."

"I thought she was Grant's fiancé?" He seemed confused.

"Oh, she might be," replied Maggie cryptically. "Now, hold still. This could hurt a bit." She cut away at the stitches. "I keep prayin' my sons will find decent women to settle with. I know He won't let me down."

"Your prayers are wasted on me, Ma."

She looked pragmatic. "I doubt that. Hard cases such as yourself seem to require extra prayers. It'll take a bit longer, but I've got nothin' but time."

He snorted in reply, as his eyes roamed over me. I could not help wondering what he was thinking.

Manufactured by Amazon.ca
Bolton, ON